Sweet Victory: A Romantic Comedy

The Dartmouth Diaries Book Two

Beverley Watts

BaR Publishing

Contents

Chapter One

It was just over a year since Hollywood had descended on the small yachting haven of Dartmouth, and after all the excitement, things had very much returned to normal.

In fact, as far as Admiral Charles Shackleford (Retired) was concerned, nothing had changed at all. Except for one thing…

Ensconced on his favourite bar stool in the Ship Inn, he sighed irritably, and stared down into his pint. Where the bloody hell was Jimmy?

Since the shenanigans in London, his best friend had had a right wendy on. In fact, though he would never admit it to a soul, the Admiral would almost have given away his beloved Admiralty to have things the way they used to be. He sighed again, this time bemoaning things lost. His former Master At Arms had got a taste of freedom and wasn't likely to be put back in his box any time soon. Of course, it was all down to that dragon Jimmy lived with, and nothing at all to do with a certain retired officer interfering in affairs that were none of his concern.

Sighing for the third time, Charles Shackleford reflected on the ungratefulness of people. After all, it had all turned out toppers in the end.

Except for the fact that nothing else had changed. Victory was still living at home – most of the time, when she wasn't up to her elbows in builder's dust up at Noah's place. But the Yank still hadn't popped the question. The Admiral frowned. He thought he could just move Tory out and Mabel in. Problem was, it wasn't turning out to be quite so simple. Mabel wanted him to make an honest woman of her. Flatly refused to leave her cosy cottage for his "mausoleum" unless she had a ring on her finger.

Now he wasn't averse to marrying Mabel – she was a much better cook than Victory – but how could he possibly have a wedding before his own daughter?

And that was the crux of the matter. Although it grieved him to admit it, he needed to ask Jimmy's advice – except that his friend had gone decidedly lily livered since that slight hiccup with Victory and Noah last year.

Suddenly, the door to the Ship opened, bringing with it a blast of fresh air, and, much to the Admiral's relief, the small figure of Jimmy – along with Pickles who had apparently been sitting patiently outside in the porch for the last twenty minutes.

'Sorry I'm late, Sir,' Jimmy breathed, hurriedly divesting himself of his coat on the way to the bar. 'Had a few things to do with Emily this morning.'

Admiral Shackleford resisted the urge to ask exactly what could be more important than their Friday lunchtime drink - mostly because he was actually worried that Jimmy might tell him. He contented himself with a frown and a slight sniff. At least his friend hadn't gone completely AWOL, and still understood the importance of recognising rank.

Signalling to the barmaid to bring another pint for himself and one for Jimmy, the Admiral waited impatiently for the smaller man to climb onto his bar stool and get settled. In the end, his impatience got the better of him. 'What the bloody hell are you doing, Jimmy?' he demanded irritably, as Jimmy continued to shuffle his bottom. 'You look like a trained monkey.'

Glancing up at his friend's crotchety face, Jimmy nevertheless persisted with his fidgeting, until eventually, settled to his satisfaction, he leaned forward and picked his beer up from the bar. 'Got the stool with the rip in,' he finally responded mildly before taking a long draft of his pint.

The Admiral had never wanted to turn the clock back more than at that particular moment. A year ago, such an offhand comment would have resulted in Jimmy doing four days dishwasher duty. That bloody woman he was married to had a lot to answer for. Taking a hasty swallow of his own beer, the Admiral stemmed his rising frustration, reminding himself that he needed his friend's help.

Placing his pint decisively back on the bar, the Admiral took a deep breath. 'The thing is Jimmy lad, I've got a bit of a situation and, even though you're usually as much use as tits on a bull, it has to be said that two brains focusing on the problem are much better than one.'

Jimmy put his own drink back on the bar and turned towards the Admiral with a frown. What the hell had the silly bugger got himself involved in now? He was tempted to tell the conniving old shark exactly what he could do with his situation, but at the end of the day, old habits really do die hard, and, as much as he'd promised Emily that he wouldn't get drawn into any more of the Admiral's harebrained schemes, he heard himself saying, 'What can I do for you, Sir?'

'That's the spirit, Jimmy,' the Admiral responded enthusiastically, causing Jimmy's heart to plummet in alarm. 'See, even though I was selflessly instrumental in bringing Noah and Victory together...' Jimmy's look of complete incredulity caused him to falter slightly, but after a short pause, he coughed and ploughed on determinedly, '...it occurred to me that they are not yet *exactly* together.' He halted expectantly, waiting for Jimmy to acknowledge his superior observational skills. Instead, he watched his friend go an interesting shade of purple while making peculiar strangling sounds.

Just when he was about to ask if the cat had got his tongue, the Admiral jumped as Jimmy leaped off the stool shouting, 'Are you out of your mi...?' only to be cut off as he landed straight on top of Pickles's tail. The elderly Springer, who'd been dozing contentedly at their feet, took off like a sprightly two-year-old, leaving Jimmy poleaxed at Charles Shackleford's feet.

Ignoring his dog who was now sitting shivering behind the bar, the Admiral stared down in astonishment at his friend lying stunned in front of him. 'What the bollocking hell's wrong with you today, man? You're acting like a lost fart in a haunted milk bottle. Have you been on the hard stuff?'

Staring up at the red-veined face directly above him, Jimmy opened his mouth, but nothing came out. It had to be said, he actually felt a bit lightheaded – not surprising really as he'd cracked his head on the edge of the stool on his way down. Gingerly feeling around the back of his skull for a lump, he managed to sit up with absolutely no help from the Admiral who was still staring at him as though he were a particularly bizarre form of aquatic life.

Finally, staggering to his feet, Jimmy clambered shakily back onto his stool while trying to gather his scattered wits together. Charles Shackleford shook his head at his friend's apparent clumsiness as he handed him his pint with a nod towards its amber contents. 'Drink that lad, it'll put you back on your feet. Can't think what's got into you today. Lucky the pub's not full. PICKLES...' The last was shouted at the top of his voice, causing Jimmy to wince and close his eyes. Appearing round the corner of the bar looking sheepish but none the worse for wear, Pickles gingerly returned to his earlier spot, keeping a wary eye out for any further falling limbs.

'So, Jimmy boy,' the Admiral continued, completely dismissing his friend's recent brush with possible death or at least the odd broken bone. 'Bottom line is, I want to marry Mabel but can't do it while our Victory's still not hitched. What do you think? I'm counting on you. In the words of Black Adder, we need to come up with a plan so cunning you could stick a tail on it and call it a fox…'

Chapter Two

Hang on a minute, Dotty. I'll be with you in a couple of seconds. Just don't christen the fifteen-thousand-pound Persian rug in the meantime.' Hurriedly, I finish attaching the last hook onto the curtain rail and clamber down the stepladder to let the little dog out into the garden. Smiling, I watch her immediately dash off in a flurry of excited barking towards a particularly large crow sitting eyeing her disdainfully from the fence. Then, as she disappears from view, I turn back to survey my handiwork.

Fourteen months, one week and three days after starting this project, Noah's house is finally beginning to look like a home. I've just finished hanging the last of the curtains up to the enormous bi-fold doors leading out onto the newly constructed porch and terrace beyond, and, though I say so myself, the room really is beautiful. Decorated in soft pastel blues and greys so reminiscent of the British seaside, the drawing room seems to echo the ever-changing moods of the ocean. It hardly resembles the one I sat in so many months ago while trying to convince Noah Westbrook, aka gorgeous Hollywood superstar, to let me be his decorator. Taking a chance on an unknown is typical of the enigma that is Noah. And, of course, falling in love with one is too.

Sighing I pick up the step ladders and take them into the utility room. My arms are aching after holding heavy fabric in the air for so long, and I rub them absently as I wander back into the bright shiny state-of-the-art kitchen.

The last year has been an amazing roller coaster. Working on the house in between travelling to see Noah on location as he finished filming *The Bridegroom*, dodging the paparazzi, and culminating in the premier in Leicester Square. The film has been a huge success, helping to cement Noah's status as the most in-demand actor in the world.

The problem is, I don't know where that leaves me. His house is practically finished. His house. I don't need a ring, I really don't, but it's difficult loving someone who everyone wants a piece of, especially when I can in no way compete. I know I sound whiny, ungrateful, not to mention downright pathetic, and when Noah and I are together, everything is fine.

It's when we're apart that the uncertainties rear their ugly heads, and right now, that's most of the time. I haven't actually seen Noah since the premier nearly six weeks ago. He's off filming his latest blockbuster – a sci-fi thriller. Still, apparently, they're going to be on location in Ireland over the next few weeks, so at least we'll only have the Irish sea separating us, and hopefully we might grab some private time together.

Dotty's barking and scratching at the door pulls me out of my maudlin reverie, and I make a concerted effort to pull myself together as I go to let her back in. Live for the present, I tell myself sternly and stop analyzing everything to the *n*th degree…

As I open the door, my mobile phone rings, and looking down, I smile as Kit's name comes up on the screen. I haven't seen my best friend for over a week as she's been off on one of her buying trips for the gallery.

'Hey, Kitty Kat, how's it going, you back?' I ask, closing the door as Dotty comes shooting in.

'Yeah, home safe and sound,' she responds, 'I cut the trip short to get back into Dartmouth before the madness of Regatta week and no parking spaces within a ten-mile radius.' She pauses, then goes on carefully, 'Will Noah be coming back for the Regatta?'

'Doubtful,' is my glum response.

'Then we'll just have to party without him.' Kit's tone, as always, pulls me out of my down-in-the-dumps mood, and I can't help but picture the mischief we've got up to in previous regattas over the years.

Dartmouth Royal Regatta Sailing week is arguably one the UK's oldest sailing regattas. It's definitely one of the most popular, and the town is usually crammed throughout the week for the various onshore and offshore entertainment. Basically, a whole week of total chaos…

Smiling, I ask if she's crewing for Ben Sheppherd this year.

'Don't think so, haven't seen him for a while. Not even sure he's racing this year. Rumour has it, he's split up with his wife and taking it pretty bad.'

'Wow, bummer. I thought they were really good together. He absolutely idolized her. If you see him, tell him how sorry I am.' Then, determinedly changing the subject from couples splitting up, 'So, how did the shopping go?'

'Pretty successful. I managed to bag some nice goodies for the lead up to Christmas. Just don't like thinking about it in August.'

'Hear, hear,' I respond resolutely refusing to think about Christmas and exactly where Noah and I will be then.

'You fancy exchanging your ivory palace in progress for the cosy delights of the Cherub and a bottle of wine?' As usual, Kit immediately senses my anxiety and takes the best possible steps to alleviate it. What on earth would I do without her?

'Sounds good.' I smile down the phone before glancing down at my watch and adding, 'Early doors?'

'Perfect, see you there at six. We'll discuss our plans for the Regatta. It's only two weeks away. Me thinks we might need some chips, you know, added brain power...'

Laughing I put down the phone, my good humour restored. 'Come on, Dotspot, our shift's over for the day.' Dotty looks up from her frenzied back scratching on said fifteen-thousand-pound rug, before rolling over and doing a bit of enthusiastic digging. I can't help but wince a little as I hurriedly pick her up. Good job Noah's not too house proud.

After checking everything's okay, I set the alarm before heading out of the front door. As I walk towards my car parked a little way down the narrow road, I pause and turn back to view the small section of Noah's house that's visible from the road. It really is a hidden gem. To anyone passing, it appears to be a small bungalow set on the side of the road, but that impression is completely misleading. The vast majority of the house is completely concealed from the road and is set into the hillside with its garden stretching down towards the beautiful River Dart.

Turning back to my car, I unlock the door and put Dotty on the back seat. As I make my way round to the driver's side, her sudden excited barking makes me jump, and I look up to see a familiar figure making his way from under some trees down the road.

Sighing, I lean back against the driver's door. 'Hello, Harry, how long have you been lurking in the bushes?'

'Not long,' comes the cheerful reply. 'Only a couple of hours.'

'You do know that Noah's not here, don't you?' Harry freelances for one of the more lurid tabloids, but unlike most of the paparazzi, he actually seems nice. We've had several in-depth discussions about the sorry state of journalism today and most of the pictures he's taken of me have actually been quite flattering – in fact I think he might even have airbrushed a couple...

'I know. He's on his way to Al Massira airport in Morocco as we speak,' he responds with a dismissive wave of his hand. I shake my head ruefully in recognition that the small man knows more about my beloved's whereabouts than I do. 'It's actually you I wanted to speak to.' I frown at the unaccustomed seriousness in his voice, and my heart thuds painfully in my chest.

I resist the urge to jump in the car and drive away as something in his tone tells me I don't really want to hear what he has to say. Instead, I offer him a lift down into Kingswear, my heart beating faster as he nods his head solemnly and walks round to the passenger side without saying anything else.

For the next few moments, the only sound in the car is me as I start the engine, and Dotty as she throws herself joyfully into Harry's lap. That's another reason why I like him. Dotty's a very good judge of character. As I wind my way carefully down the road towards Kingswear, I risk glancing over at him, just as he raises his head to look over at me. This time, my heart lurches sickeningly as I witness the sympathy in his gaze.

Not again, please, please, not again.

I turn my eyes determinedly back to the road as I wait for him to tell me that Noah has been caught in a compromising position with one of the bevy of beautiful women that hover around him like bees round a honeypot. To my surprise, his first words aren't about Noah at all. 'Word on the streets is they've dug up some dirt on your old man.' I pull a face as his words sink in. 'What, like he was possibly the worst two star ever to grace the Royal Navy's wall of fame? I think that's common knowledge, sunshine.'

'Trust me Tory, it's much worse than that. God knows how, but they've unearthed a retired Thai prostitute who says your father murdered her husband.'

I'm on my second glass of wine, and I'm only now beginning to calm down. Harry didn't know the full story, only that the incident allegedly happened when my father was a lowly Lieutenant.

After dropping Harry off at the Passenger Ferry in Kingswear, I drove round to the Admiralty like I was auditioning for Brands Hatch, but there was no sign of my father, or Pickles for that matter. I tried his mobile phone but like always, it was switched off. In the end, I called Kit to tell her that I wasn't feeling well and wouldn't be coming over to the Cherub, poured myself a large glass of wine, and sat down in his study to wait.

My mind is now racing. How on earth could my bluff, bighearted, irresponsible father possibly have murdered anybody? God knows I've been tempted to do him in myself a few times. Un-PC he might be, but a murderer, never. And what the hell was he doing getting involved with a Thai prostitute (well obviously I *do* know, but still...) And anyway, wasn't he with mum by the time he joined the Royal Navy... Oh God, I'm just going round in circles. I daren't even think about how this is going to affect Noah.

Suddenly, my endless head chatter is interrupted by the sound of a door opening. I know it's the Admiral because Dotty is beside herself with happiness (at seeing Pickles, not my father...) I stand nervously, gripping my half empty glass like a lifeline and wait for him to open the study door.

'Victory,' he shouts as he stomps across the hall, obviously nearly falling over Pickles in the process if the sudden crash and, 'Bloody hell dog, you'll have me arse over tit in a minute,' is anything to go by. 'Vict....' He stutters to a halt as he throws open the study door and sees me standing there. It's so unusual for him to find me in his personal sanctuary that for a couple of seconds he's actually lost for words. Then, taking in my white face and stiff posture, he turns and closes the door before saying in an uncharacteristically mild tone, 'Do I need a drop of the hard stuff before we start?'

I nod, not trusting myself to speak. I can tell he thinks this is all about Noah. He has absolutely no idea of the bombshell I'm about to drop. I sit down and try to compose myself as he helps himself to a glass of port. Even Dotty and Pickles sense that something is wrong as they sit side by side on the rug and stare anxiously at us both.

'Right then.' His voice is matter of fact as he plonks himself in his chair opposite. 'Come on girl, spit it out. Has the Yank dumped you or what?'

I shake my head, for once completely oblivious to his less-than-gentle method of questioning. 'No, well, not yet anyway.' I hold my hand up as he tries to interrupt, and continue breathlessly, 'It's not about Noah, Dad. It's about you.' At his frown, I take a large gulp of my wine and finish in a rush, 'Dad, they're saying you killed a Thai prostitute, well not a prostitute exactly, but the husband of one. You didn't, did you? You couldn't possibly have done something like that could you? I mean what were you doing in Thailand, and why would you have anything to do with a prostitute, or the husband of one? Weren't you and mum married by then?' I splutter to a halt, the sick feeling intensifying in my stomach as I take in his stillness and sudden pallor.

The silence lengthens. 'Dad?' I whisper, fear clogging my throat at his failure to answer. 'Please, Dad, you have to talk to me. It's going to be all over the news by the weekend.' For a few more seconds, I actually think he's not going to answer, and I have to resist the urge to get up and shake him. Then he sighs and closes his eyes briefly before swallowing his glass of port in one go.

Finally, he looks across at me. 'I didn't kill anyone, Victory, nobody did. It was an accident.' And, despite my best efforts, he refuses to say another word.

Daylight is beginning to fade into dusk outside as Dad and I continue to sit in silence. According to Harry, the story will break in the next couple of days, and I want to scream and shout at my father, beg him to come clean and tell the world what really happened, but I know how he works. Begging and pleading will get me nowhere. So instead, I do nothing, simply stare into my now-empty glass and wish I could drown my sorrows in the rest of the bottle.

'I need to speak to Jimmy.' His sudden announcement makes me jump, and I look up as he stands to fish his mobile phone out of his pocket.

'Why?' I ask bluntly. 'Is he involved in this mess too?' My father's answer is to raise his eyebrows and frown at me until sighing. I climb reluctantly out of my chair and turn on the lamps. I need to speak to Noah too, as soon as possible. Trouble is, I can't bring myself to do it just yet. I have no idea what he'll say. Leaving Dad to his phone call, I head to the kitchen to sort out dog food and make some sandwiches - mostly as something solid to soak up the wine (the sandwiches that is, not the dog food...)

My mind stays blessedly numb as I focus determinedly on the mundane actions of spreading and cutting, and when my father pushes open the kitchen door ten minutes later, I'm surprised to note that I've used up nearly a whole loaf of bread. 'Bollocking hell, Victory. We might have a bit of a problem, but we're not on the verge of a bloody famine.' I stare down at the knife in my hand and grit my teeth. A bit of a problem? I'll give him a bit of a problem...

Leaning down to grab one of the sandwiches, my father waves

it at me before taking a large appreciative bite, completely oblivious to my murderous thoughts. 'Everything's going to be shipshape, Victory, don't you worry. Thing is, they can't prove anything.' The breadcrumbs spraying everywhere are the least of my worries as I stare incredulously at him. 'Nobody was done in, it's all just a big misunderstanding. All we need to do is lie low for a bit, and it'll all blow over, you'll see.'

Obviously, my completely deluded parent has recovered from his brief spell of vulnerability and is now firmly back in cloud cuckoo land. 'Dad, they are going to hang you out to dry. Can't you see that?' My voice has risen to a shout, and I take a deep breath in an effort to calm down. 'The police will want to question you,' I continue more evenly. 'You won't be able to lie low anywhere. You could even go to prison. We're talking about a murder, Dad, not just a one-day wonder of an ex-Admiral shagging a hooker forty years ago...'

He sighs, looking for all the world as though I'm the problem. 'You don't need to worry,' he says again, slowly this time. 'I'll turn myself in, they'll let me out on bail, and then we'll hole up somewhere quiet until it's all sorted.' I gawp at him in complete disbelief at his naivety. 'So what exactly are you going to say happened, Dad? How are you going to explain it? You said it was an accident.'

'Aye, it was,' he responds firmly. 'But I won't be breathing a word of what happened to you or anyone else.' Then he glares at me with uncharacteristic steel and, for the first time ever, I see a glimmer of the qualities that got him promoted to Admiral. 'I'll sort this bloody mess out, Victory, and I don't want you involved. I mean it, you leave this to me. If you so much as stick your little toe into this mess, I will no longer call you my daughter.' And with that he grabs another sandwich, calls to Pickles and disappears out of the door.

∞∞∞

Most of the pub's regulars had gone by the time the Admiral arrived at the Ship, although there were still a few die-hard tourists sitting outside making the most of the last of the sun's rays in the deepening twilight. It had taken him exactly seventeen minutes to get here which he thought might actually be a record.

Pausing to get his breath back, he looked round the nearly empty bar and immediately spotted Jimmy nursing his beer in the corner. The smaller man was irritably wondering why the Admiral had insisted they meet for a drink just as CSI was about to start on the TV. He'd nearly refused to come, especially as Emily had only a minute ago brought out some cheese and pickles for supper, but something in the Admiral's voice had made him hesitate, and, after assuring his wife that he'd only stay for a quick pint, he swallowed his sudden apprehension and hurried round the corner to the Ship.

'So, what's this all about, Sir?' Jimmy asked brusquely once the Admiral had ordered a pint and settled himself in the seat opposite. 'You're surely not serious about meddling in Tory's business again, are you?' The Admiral frowned at his friend's choice of words – if he hadn't "meddled" nearly forty years ago, things would be looking very different now and he'd a good mind to tell him so. Then he sighed. It wouldn't do either of them any good to start throwing stones this late in the day.

'I wish that's all it was, Jimmy lad, but our Victory's love life is the least of our worries at the moment. In fact, I'm pretty certain she won't even have one once everything comes out. No, I'm afraid this is about you and me, Jim, and what I'm about to tell you will be as welcome as a fart in a spacesuit.'

The Admiral paused, unable to continue as he watched the

15

colour drain from his friend's face. Stalling for time, he took a long draft of his pint, and decided that the only way to break the news of the impending disaster was to just come out with it.

Placing the glass carefully back on the table in front of him, he raised his eyes back to Jimmy's stricken ones. His oldest friend knew what was coming.

'The Hermes problem's finally surfaced again,' he said bluntly, finally, 'and the cat is well and truly out of the bag this time.'

An hour later, the two men parted ways outside the pub. The Admiral stood for a second, watching his friend's bent shoulders and slow steps with an unexpectedly heavy heart. He'd believed he'd give anything to have his relationship with Jimmy back to the way it used to be.

But not this, never this.

∞∞∞

It's eleven o'clock at night. My mobile phone keeps ringing. Noah and Kit. Both are probably worried sick about me by now. I text Kit, still keeping up the pretence of a sudden virus, promising I'll call her tomorrow. She knows something fishy's going on, but what exactly am I going to tell her? Will she believe my father's capable of murder?

But whatever happens, I have to tell Noah. I owe him that much, and Dad knows it. Of course, there's no way we can be together after this. It could completely ruin his career. Although come to think of it, Hugh Grant got away with being involved with a lady of the night, and it even enhanced his career – although it has to be said he didn't actually murder either her or any of her family, so I suppose it's not *quite* the same.

I roll over and cuddle Dotty to me. She's snoring happily,

completely oblivious to the disaster looming – oh to be a dog...

I know I can't put it off any longer. Sitting up, I shuffle backwards until I'm leaning against the bed headboard and dial Noah's number...

...Only to have it go straight to answer phone. I dial again and listen to Noah's sexy voice telling me to leave a message. And again. And again. By now, I'm getting completely frantic. How on earth can I tell him everything by answer phone? Why the bloody hell didn't I just answer the phone when he called? In the end I ask him to ring me as soon as he gets my message. Then just as I disconnect the call, I see a red light flashing, indicating I have a message of my own. Almost crying with relief, I guess we're playing answer phone ping pong and press the button to listen.

'Hi babe, sorry I missed you, but wanted to let you know I'll have no signal over the next couple days as we're filming in the hills of Tenerife. Will try and get to a landline to call you when I can but as we're well and truly roughing it, could be the weekend before I manage it. Missing you Tor, won't be long until we're together again, I promise. Take care gorgeous, love you loads.'

I feel sick.

Chapter Three

After the fifth time calling Tory's number, Noah was forced to leave a message in case he lost the signal. A short time later, after checking again, it was gone. Sighing, he leant back against the seat of the luxury coach they were travelling in. It was already dark outside, twilight coming early and suddenly this near to the equator.

Noah hated this kind of inactivity. Not speaking to Tory had left him on edge. He hoped she was okay. It had been tough the last few weeks, and he knew the separation was getting to both of them. Tory wasn't used to living in the limelight and hated the constant presence of the paparazzi, the speculation and bitchy, vindictive comments that appeared with unfailing regularity on the internet and in the entertainment magazines. He'd yet to take her over to California to meet his sister and her family which would have gone a long way to showing her just how normal his background was. Filming commitments had gotten in the way, and he didn't think they'd get time to visit with Kim and Ben until this movie was finished.

His musings were cut short by the arrival of his latest female co-star. Unlike Gaynor, there was no history between them – in fact they'd never met before the set of this movie. Laurel Price was a dark sultry beauty proclaiming her roots were in the Middle East. However, despite her looks, she was British through and through, having grown up on a council estate in Leeds and declaring herself, 'A proud Yorkshire lass right through to me knickers.' Also, unlike Gaynor, she had no airs and graces, no prima donna tendencies and considered herself just one of the crew. She'd done her time in British TV dramas and was now on the cusp of superstardom. Her first major movie role with Noah Westbrook was her agent's wildest dream.

'Did you manage to get through?' she asked, seating herself next to him. Noah simply shook his head, not in the mood for an extended conversation. As likeable as Laurel was, he quickly realized she'd talk for England given half a chance.

'I'm sure she's fine,' Laurel went on, completely ignoring his disinclination to talk. She and Tory had met a couple of times during the course of filming and luckily got on like a house on fire, which was a real bonus considering the usual tabloid speculations about male and female leads extending their on-screen chemistry off screen - especially after the craziness of *The Bridegroom.*

Noah knew she was probably right, but for some reason he was anxious. It didn't help that he'd had a conversation with his own agent earlier who made no bones about the fact that he believed Tory was bad for his career.

'Your fans want you single. They need to believe they've all got the same kinda chance as Tory. You've gotten everything you're gonna get out of that relationship, Noah. You need to bail.'

Noah had no intention of giving Tory up. She was the most important thing in his life right now, and, although he hadn't yet said so to his agent, if it came to choosing between them, he would bail on his career before he let Victory go. However, this was a conversation he knew was coming, and unbeknown to Tim, he'd already made discreet enquires about moving to a different agent – one who wasn't quite so single-mindedly ruthless.

The coach was going tortuously slow, winding its way around the hair-raisingly narrow road up into the foothills towards Mount Teide and the bizarre lunar landscape that made Tenerife so popular for makers of science fiction movies. For once Laurel seemed content to let the silence continue, and after giving her a quick grateful smile, Noah closed his eyes, smothered his unease and tried to get some sleep.

It's six o'clock in the morning and I haven't slept a wink all night. Despite endless scenarios playing themselves in full technicolour inside my head, I'm no closer to coming up with some kind of a solution to our *bit of a problem*. All I can think about is speaking to Noah before someone else does, and getting the hell out of Dartmouth before the shit completely hits the fan.

By six thirty, I give up trying to sleep and, much to Dotty's disgust, I climb out of bed and throw open the curtains. It's a beautiful day. How can it be a beautiful day when I'm about to become notorious – and for all the wrong reasons?

Heading downstairs in my dressing gown, I leave Dotty snoozing, knowing she'll come down when her bladder's unable to hang on any longer. There's no sign of my father or Pickles, leaving me to assume he's not had any sleep either. I put the kettle on and seat myself at the kitchen table while I wait for it to boil. My stomach roils queasily at the thought of eating anything, so I close my eyes, and for a few seconds lose myself in the fantasy that it's all a big mistake and my father is not about to become responsible for the biggest naval scandal since Admiral Nelson got involved with "that Hamilton woman". I'm just getting to the part where Noah and I are laughing about the silliness of it all, when I'm brought back to reality by the sound of barking in the front garden.

Recognising Pickles, I jump up and open the door. Wagging his tail furiously, the elderly Springer dashes in, and I leave the door open, knowing my father will appear at some point. Just as I finish the process of making tea – the Englishman's choice of beverage in a crisis (and mine when it's too early for a glass of wine), Dotty comes tearing into the kitchen, all thoughts of a lie-in forgotten with the arrival of her hero. I smile as I see them dance around each other before dashing back out into the garden. Picking up my cup, I take my tea and stand in the open doorway, watching them play.

It's a truly beautiful day, so typical of early August. Sipping my tea, I stand and stare at the amazing panorama laid out before me. The sunlight is dancing on the River Dart and shimmering over the hills behind. All is silent apart from the muted noise of the car ferry, nearly empty at this time in the morning. The whole thing seems so surreal. My life is falling apart, and yet everything looks exactly the same.

I'm so scared that Noah will hear the sordid details before I have a chance to speak to him, but then, does it really matter? Maybe it will actually work out better if he believes the worst from the off. It will make it much easier to walk away.

'You keep telling yourself that, Victory Shackleford.' My inner voice is scathing, but luckily, I'm saved from listening to it for long by the dulcet tones of my father yelling from the other side of the shiny new gates that protect us from the road behind the house. 'VICTORY, THE BLOODY MUTT HAS LOCKED ME OUT AGAIN.' The massive gates had come courtesy of *The Bridegroom*. Designed to protect us against anything from an influx of reporters to an avalanche, their only problem is a tendency to slam shut behind anyone, man or beast, who pushes them open too forcefully. I know my father has a habit of leaving them ajar when he goes out – mostly because he always forgets to take the remote control with him. Heading back into the kitchen to look for it, I reflect it's one habit he's definitely going to have to ditch or we're likely to be overrun with paparazzi hiding in our flower beds.

Two minutes later, he appears at the back door. He looks as though he's slept in his clothes, but then I wonder if he's actually been to bed. I open my mouth to ask if he's okay, but his next words stop me in my tracks.

'Right then, get your bags packed, Victory. We're heading north.' His tone is definitely not that of a man condemned, and my heart lifts slightly as I wonder if he's actually found a way to wriggle out of the mess we're in.

'Where are we going?'

'Scotland. Chap I served with on Hermes in the seventies. Owes me a favour. His family's got this pile o' bricks on the banks of Loch Long, middle of nowhere. Spot on it is – nobody will look for us there.'

I stare at him in disbelief. 'Let me get this straight, Dad. You expect me to just up sticks and drive five hundred miles to some mausoleum out in the sticks based on the advice from some bloke you knew back in the seventies? That's your plan?'

He actually nods his head in apparent approval at my succinct summing up of the situation. 'That's about the right of it. I've already told Mabel and she's agreed to look after Pickles while we're away. Thought you'd want to take the mongrel with you.' He waits for me to say something else, but for once I'm completely lost for words. Taking my silence for agreement, he slaps his hand on the table enthusiastically before saying, 'Well, come on then, show a leg girl, we need to be on the road by teatime.'

I swear to God he's actually enjoying this. 'STOP,' I shout as he's about to throw open the kitchen door, causing him to turn round in surprise.

'I am not going to simply climb in a car with you and drive to God knows where without some more information.' Frowning, he heads back to the kitchen table. 'What else do you want to know?' he asks in his "Victory's being a pain in the arse again" tone of voice.

I take a deep breath. 'Well for starters, exactly who is this person whose family owns a mansion in Scotland?'

'Hugo Buchannan. We go back a long way. To be fair, always thought he was a bit of a pickle jar officer...' He pauses at my look of complete incomprehension before hurriedly clarifying, 'You know the sort of mamby pamby graduate who could tell you the square root of a pickle jar lid to three decimal places but can't get the bloody thing off.

'Anyway, turned out to be a bit of a flyer. Would have gone far too except his dad happened to pop his clogs and old Hugo had to go back home to take over the family estate. He's on his own now. Think his wife died about the same time as your mother.'

'So, what is this favour he owes you exactly?' I ask suspiciously when it becomes clear my father's finished his explanation. He raises his eyes to the ceiling and sighs before saying irritably. 'I can't tell you that Victory, if I did, he wouldn't owe me a favour anymore now, would he?'

'So that's it then, you're not going to tell me. Is it another murder you're covering up? I mean, how many are there? And what's to stop good old Mr. Hugo Buchannan from telling the world where we are?' My voice is getting louder, the sarcasm gradually being replaced by bubbling hysteria.

'Don't be so bloody melodramatic, Victory,' is my father's exasperated response, cutting me off in midrant. 'Hugo and I have a gentleman's agreement. That's all you need to know, and for the last bollocking time, nobody's murdered anybody. Now, are you coming with me to Scotland, or are you going to sit here and knit while everything goes tits up around you?'

I open my mouth to protest some more but realize there's really nothing else to say. I can feel the tears threatening behind my eyes. It's all so bloody unfair. Swallowing the sudden lump in my throat, I nod my head. 'I need to tell Kit and Freddy that I'm leaving.' I climb wearily out of my chair and turn towards the door.

'What about Noah?' My father's blunt question stops me in my tracks and without turning round, I answer softly, 'I haven't been able to speak to him yet. I'll try to fill him in before the tabloids get hold of him, but, well, whatever happens, we both know it's over.'

It's nearly midday by the time I get a chance to send a quick text to both Kit and Freddy, telling them I need to see them both urgently. To save time I head straight over to the gallery, hoping and praying Kit's not too busy to talk. Freddy's response is gratifyingly quick, but I still haven't heard back from Kit by the time the ferry's deposited me on the other side, which doesn't bode well. As I cut through the park and walk past the bandstand, I can't help but remember the Music Festival here over a year ago now. I smile as I remember my complete and utter amazement at the thought that Noah Westbrook might actually want more from me than a quick bonk...

Ruthlessly pushing down the memories, I pick Dotty up and hurry out of the park, fighting my way past the hordes of tourists enjoying the summer sunshine. By the time I turn into Foss Street, I'm hot, sweaty and want nothing more than to sit in a darkened room with a bottle of wine and a straw...

The gallery is thankfully empty as I enter its cool dim interior with relief. Hoping that Kit will understand, I immediately shut the door behind me and hang the closed sign on it. I can hear Kit's voice in the back office, and putting Dotty back onto the floor, I start to push open the door just as she begins to shout.

Surprised, I stop dead. Kit *never* shouts.

'You know what mum? You can do whatever you damn well like with it. I'm done.' The sound of swearing jerks me out of my sudden trance, and I hurriedly open the door, only to duck quickly as the phone comes sailing past my shoulder. As she catches sight of me, my best friend bursts into tears, and I rush forward, all thoughts of my own problems forgotten.

Enfolding her unresisting body in my arms, I let her cry, finally murmuring, 'Hey, Kitty Kat, what is it - what's wrong?' as she eventually subsides into tearful hiccups. Taking a deep shuddering breath, Kit looks up at me. 'That was my mum. They're selling the gallery, Tory. What am I going to do...?'

Shocked, I stare at her speechlessly. The gallery is Kit's life. It means everything to her. How on earth could her parents sell it out from under her? I really have no idea what to say, so I simply hold her to me until she finally takes a step back and fumbles for a tissue to wipe her eyes. 'You look terrible,' I say with a sympathetic smile.

'Piss off,' is Kit's response, telling me she's done with crying. 'Wine, I think,' she continues after blowing her nose. She turns determinedly towards the filing cabinet where everything alcoholic is kept and for a second, I'm silent, the thought of a drink oh so appealing when everything seems to be going to rats. Then I think of the drive tonight. There's no way I'm sitting in the passenger seat for five hundred miles with a man who's attended so many driver improvement courses, he's on first name terms with most of the traffic police in Devon.

'Not for me, Kit, I've got a long drive to do in a few hours.' Frowning, she turns back towards me. 'Why, where are you going?'

And so, I tell her.

Halfway through, Freddy arrives, so I'm forced to go over the whole improbable story again as my two best friends knock back a bottle of wine while staring at me as though I've suddenly sprouted two heads (or become the daughter of a murderous criminal…)

'So, that's pretty much it,' I finish at length. 'We've got to lie low for a week or so until the whole thing sorts itself out.'

'How on earth is it going to do that?' Kit asks, voicing the same question that's been rattling around in my head for nearly two days.

'I've no idea,' I respond wearily, truthfully. 'All I know is my father says everything will be okay, and I have to believe him. It's not like he's never got himself in a difficult position before.'

'Bit different to being pulled over for speeding though,' is Freddy's wonderfully helpful comment.'

'What have you told Noah?' Kit finally asks the question I've been dreading, and I close my eyes against the sudden prick of tears.

'Nothing yet. I haven't managed to speak to him. He'll be out of contact until the weekend. Who's taking bets on whether I get to speak to him before the media tracks him down?' My attempt at a lighthearted quip is met with deafening silence, and I know exactly what they're both thinking.

'I know this will finish us,' I say quietly. 'I'm not stupid. There's no way we can stay together after this. The tabloids will have a field day. It will ruin his career.'

'You don't know that,' Kit argues half-heartedly as I shake my head. 'It doesn't matter. I won't let him give up everything he's worked so hard for. I'd just like him to know my side of things before I end it. I'll keep trying to get hold of him as we head north.'

'So where exactly are you staying?' Freddy asks, tactfully redirecting the subject.

'I can't tell you,' I answer apologetically. 'Dad's sworn me to secrecy. And of course, what you don't know, they can't torture you to reveal.' Kit drains her glass and stands up.

'They won't have to because I'm coming with you.' I gawp at her. It's the last thing I expect her to say. 'What about the gallery?' I finally manage as a sudden warmth unexpectedly begins to spread from my chest.

'Sod the gallery. I'll just shut up shop. Haven't you heard? They're selling the bloody thing anyway.' She smiles broadly at me, and I can't help but smile back.

Freddy's face is a picture. He so hates being left in the dark. I expect him to demand an explanation from Kit, but all he says is, 'Bloody hell, the last time I had this much excitement was when I bumped into Ricky Martin in Harrods. Of course, I'm coming too. I'm owed some holiday. Just give me a couple of hours to sort out cover.'

Before I can open my mouth to protest that there's no way we'll all get comfortably in Dad's Volvo, Kit gets there first. 'We'll take my seven-seater. There'll be more room.

'Of course, you'll have to drive Tory, at least until I'm legal again. There's no way I'm letting your old man sit behind the wheel of any vehicle I own.'

Before I have a chance to protest again, Freddy dashes out of the office shouting 'So exciting, it's just like Bonny and Clyde.' I sit staring after him, finally allowing the tears to spill down my cheeks.

What on earth did I do to deserve such amazing friends?

'Scotland? We're going to bloody Scotland? Could you have

picked a hiding place a bit further away perchance?' Freddy's enthusiasm seems to have waned a bit to be replaced by his usual sarcasm. 'Why can't we fly there?'

'Because I might be recognized, and we don't want anyone to know where we're headed,' I explain patiently. 'We're travelling overnight so we should be there before the morning. You can just sleep in the back of the car.'

I expect Freddy to put up more objections and ready myself to tell him he really doesn't have to come, but all he does is sigh and subside into silence.

It's now five thirty in the evening and we're sitting in the kitchen waiting for Kit to arrive with her people carrier, although who's driving her over is anybody's guess. Dad's still holed up in his study giving Jimmy last minute instructions which I assume are along the lines of, 'Do nothing and speak to nobody...' I was expecting him to put up a fight about Kit and Freddy joining us, but all he said was, 'It's not a bloody holiday you know.'

Dotty is sitting on Freddy's knee looking up at him adoringly. I've packed all her doggy stuff, and Pickles is waiting to be dropped off at Mabel's. Suddenly the little dog launches herself off Freddy's lap, barking furiously, and I squeeze my eyes shut, wincing in protest. We're certainly never likely to be burgled as long as she's around. I can hear Pickles's answering bark in the study and assume the commotion is due to Kit finally arriving with our ride, so I'm completely blindsided when the kitchen door opens and in struggles Mabel, along with a suitcase that's bigger than she is.

Freddy and I simply stare at her as she drags what looks to be a year's worth of luggage through the door. Finally collapsing on another chair, she fans her shiny face with her handbag. 'There's no way I'm sitting here worrying about you both,' she pants eventually, 'I'm coming with you.' She says the last just as my father throws open the kitchen door, and she stares defiantly up at him as if daring him to argue.

'Way to go Mabel,' I think, looking from her to my father's face which is rapidly turning a dark purple as he splutters and struggles to find a reason why she should stay in Dartmouth. In the end, Mabel wins, much to my complete surprise, and for the first time, I think she may actually be very good for him...

Half an hour later we're on the road. I'm taking the first half of the journey while Kit recovers from her earlier half a bottle of wine. She's sitting in the passenger seat though, and Dotty is quite content to curl up in her lap. My father and Mabel are sitting side by side in the middle seats, with Pickles between them. Both are looking a bit ill at ease – I think their earlier "discussion" might actually have been their first row. The back seat has been commandeered by Freddy who has already made himself comfortable with a pillow and blanket.

It's going to be a long journey...

Chapter Four

It's just after three in the morning, and we're sitting at the end of a dirt track looking up at what appears to be a massive ruin. I can see the loch beyond, glinting in the strange twilight that passes for dark this far north during the summer, but any light that might have been cast on the pile of bricks in front of me is blocked by the tangle of trees encroaching the high walls. The wind is causing the leaves to rustle and moan, cementing the whole creepy forbidding impression. I fully expect a blood curdling scream to split the air like a B-rated horror movie.

'Are you sure we're in the right place?' Freddy asks, voicing the question that we're all asking inside. My heart lifts a bit as I contemplate the possibility that we've taken a wrong turn somewhere, but my father soon crushes any burgeoning hope.

'Nope, this is definitely it. Hugo emailed me a photo.' He points to a sign dimly visible over the massive front door. 'See, it says Bloodstone Tower - that's the name of Hugo's family pile.' We all stare at him silently. 'Apparently, it was featured in *Britain's Most Haunted*,' he goes on defensively when still nobody said anything. 'That's where the photo came from.'

'You've brought us over five hundred miles to a crumbling relic with a name like Bloodstone Tower, and you never thought to tell us what to expect?' Mabel's voice is high, almost shrill, and I can't help but wonder if Dad might be having second thoughts about making an honest woman of the merry widow after spending nine hours in the car with her... Mind you, she's only saying what the rest of us are thinking. My father frowns but appears to be at a loss for words – something that seems to be happening increasingly often lately. Actually though, I don't think even he'd been expecting it to be quite this bad.

'Fact is,' he blusters eventually, 'we're all shagged out. I'm sure everything will look better in the morning.'

'It *is* the morning,' is Freddy's tight-lipped response to the strained optimism in my father's voice. 'How the bloody hell are we going to get in?'

Dad opens his mouth to speak, then subsides into silence. None of us have got any answers. I'm tempted to ask if Hugo could have left a key under the pot, but one look around my plucky companions tells me my comment is likely to get me an appropriate plucky response. A loud snore suddenly punctures the silence. Dotty really isn't a fan of anything getting in the way of her beauty sleep, and that includes a nine-hour road trip.

To be fair, the journey here wasn't so bad. Freddy only began saying, 'Are we there yet?' as we got north of Birmingham, and we had a quick break halfway at a motorway service station for burgers and chips. Mabel, Kit and Freddy stood in the queue, while Dad and I sneaked to the loo. When it was Mabel's turn to spend a penny, she was gone so long we thought she'd been abducted. Turns out she was playing a quick round of bingo on the machine outside the ladies. I'm not entirely sure that she's come to grips with the gravity of the situation.

Dusk was falling as we got back on the road, with a perfectly sober Kit now at the wheel. I kept trying to get hold of Noah once she took over and still don't know if I was glad or sorry when each call went straight to answer phone. By the time we passed Glasgow and entered the foothills of the Scottish Highlands, it was as dark as it was going to get, and the colossal mountains surrounding us were just visible as shadowy monoliths.

'Well, we can't just sit here for the next four bloody hours.' Even Kit's legendary even temper is a bit frayed, and coming back to the present, I realize it's up to me to take charge.

'Come on guys, buck up. Let's get out at least. We can stretch our legs and have a quick look round. I'm not tired yet anyway after being cooped up for so long.' I climb out of the passenger seat without waiting to see if anyone follows. Dotty jumps down reluctantly and stretches daintily before wandering over to christen the nearest patch of grass. Pickle's soft whine followed by the sound of two more doors opening a few seconds later is the only indication that my suggestion has even been heard.

'Be careful, it's a bit uneven underfoot,' I call back softly as I make my way round the side of the house following an overgrown path that I hope leads to the loch shore.

'You think?' is the only answer I get. A couple of minutes later, I'm standing on a small man-made beach staring in awe at the breathtaking, almost ethereal beauty before me. The edge of the loch is only a couple of feet away, its inky black water lapping quietly up onto the shore. Beyond the loch, shrouded in mist, majestic mountains thrust eerily into the predawn sky. I catch my breath, feeling as though I'm in another world, one where modern technology has no place; a world that has been here since the dawn of time, and will still be standing when everything else is dust. One by one the others join me, and we pay silent homage to the ancient grandeur in front of us.

'Bloody hell, Charlie didnae expect you at o'crack-sparrowfart. What time do you call this?' The voice is shockingly loud in the stillness, instantly breaking the otherworldly spell. For a second, we all turn and stare up at the indistinct shape leaning precariously out of one of the top floor windows of the house, and then Dotty and Pickles destroy what's left of the tranquility by dashing up the garden and barking frenziedly at the sound of a strange voice.

∞ ∞ ∞

At five a.m., Noah gave up trying to sleep and climbing out of his sleeping bag, unzipped his tent and ducked silently outside. Even though it was still early, the weather was already warm, giving a hint at the humid temperatures to come once the sun came up. Dressed in only his boxers, Noah sat on a rock and watched the predawn sky turn pink. This far south, daybreak was a quick affair, as though the sun couldn't wait to get started.

They had finished filming in the early hours of the morning, and although he felt completely drained, Noah had been unable to sleep, his anxiety a constant gnawing in his gut. Only one more day left in the middle of nowhere, then he'd be able to contact the outside world - or, more specifically, Tory.

Noah had no idea why he was swamped by such an uncharacteristic sense of foreboding. Maybe because it was so unusual for Tory not to pick up the phone when he called. Resting his head in his hands, he took a deep breath and willed his mind to relax.

He thought back to their first meeting. That hilarious dinner party. Noah chuckled to himself, remembering Tory's desperate face as her father committed one social faux pas after another. Although not beautiful in the accepted sense, she had a guilelessness about her that had attracted him right from the start. He'd been immersed in the shallow superficiality of the acting world for so long, with only his mother and sister to keep his feet on the ground. Tory's forthright openness had been a breath of fresh air, taking a weight off his chest that he hadn't even realized existed until she came into his life.

He loved everything about her with an intensity he hadn't thought himself capable of - from her voluptuous curves to her self-deprecating sense of humour. Tory gave his life a whole new meaning – everything simply made sense when he was with her.

With a resolve that helped to still his anxiety, Noah vowed to himself that he'd never let anyone hurt her; that he'd do whatever it took to make her happy and keep her safe…

Five minutes later, the enormous front door is dragged open with a piercing squeaking sound that has all of us covering our ears and gritting our teeth in protest. The resulting lamplight gives a vague image of a cavernous hallway, but all my attention is on the small man standing in front of me.

'Charlie Shackleford,' he booms, leading me to wonder first of all, how such a little person could have such a loud voice and, secondly, whether having a voice like a foghorn is a common trait with all officers in the Royal Navy. Then, as he turns towards me and I see him properly for the first time, I blink, and my third thought is, how can anybody have that much hair? And in that particular colour – bright shocking red. He looks like a miniature version of Stoick the Vast from *How To Train Your Dragon.*

'Hugo Buchannan, at your service, ma'am,' he bellows before embracing me in a surprisingly strong grip for such a small man. After a short hesitation, I return his hug, inexplicably feeling tears gather at the back of my eyes. Gallantly, he pretends not to notice as he turns towards the rest of our party and waits for the introductions.

'Can't say I was expecting quite so many of you,' he says cheerfully after shaking hands with everyone, 'But never mind, I'm sure I'll manage to dig out some more sheets from somewhere. So, who do we have here then?' He bends down towards Dotty who is shivering next to my feet and holds out his hand for her to sniff.

'This is Dotty, and the Springer is Pickles,' I say, wondering if Dad thought to tell our host that we would be bringing a couple of canine companions.

'Well, hello, Dotty,' he continues as the small dog licks his hand hesitantly. Pickles shows no such restraint and launches himself at Hugo with abandon. I wince as the spaniel deposits sandy mud all over his dressing gown. I really hope our host likes dogs. Luckily, he chuckles as he pushes Pickles away and says only, 'Spike's going to love you two. Come on in and make yourselves at home.'

After waving for my father and Mabel to follow our host, Freddy, Kit and I go to the car to unload the bags. As they disappear inside, I can just hear Mabel saying, 'So, Charles, am I right in saying you and Hugo Buchannan served on HMS Herpes together?' Unfortunately, my father's answer is lost as the two of them are swallowed up by the entrance hall...

A few minutes later, we discover that what we'd assumed to be a large hallway, is in fact an actual, honest-to-goodness Great Hall. For a few seconds I stand and gape, the persistent sick feeling in the pit of my stomach briefly replaced by amazement. To my untrained eyes, the floor looks to be flagstone and is covered with brightly coloured rugs to ward off the chill. There are tapestries hanging on the bare stone walls, so faded it's impossible to tell what they originally depicted, and a huge fireplace at one end. Hugo is busy piling logs into an already blazing fire, despite the fact that it's essentially still the middle of the night and the middle of summer.

'Come in and get warm,' he shouts as he hears us enter. Without turning round, he waves to a couple of sofas and an armchair that have plainly seen better days grouped around an old coffee table in front of the fireplace. I notice my father, Mabel and Pickles have already claimed the sofa to the left, so, after dumping the cases in the corner, the three of us make ourselves comfortable on the remaining one. Unsurprisingly, Dotty commandeers the chair.

As I sit on the edge of the couch, the whole situation begins to feel almost dreamlike. I'm so tired and want nothing more than to sink into a bed – any bed – and sleep until it's all over. Unfortunately, our small host is displaying no signs of showing us to our rooms, if indeed any of us have one.

'Right then, tea I think.' He claps his hands, and I half expect Lurch to appear out of a dark cobwebbed corner. However, there doesn't appear to be any servants, zombie or otherwise, and Hugo disappears off, presumably to do the honours himself.

Too tired to make conversation, I look around the room, taking in the deep-set mullioned windows revealing that dawn is not far off. The flickering light is provided by wall sconces that look as though they were put up when electricity was first discovered. Nobody speaks, exhaustion obviously taking its toll. Even my father sits staring into the fire, and I vaguely wonder if he thinks the answer to our bit of a problem might be found in its amber flames.

'Here we are, this'll perk you all up.' Hugo reappears with a tray that's nearly as big as he is. Strangely enough, perk up we do, and for the first time, I understand the British obsession with tea being the cure for all ills. Mind you, the homemade Scottish shortbread might have something to do with it. Talk about a sugar rush... After about twenty minutes however, it's plain that none of us are able to keep awake any longer and, after a particularly loud snore from Mabel, our host takes the hint and stands up to show us to our rooms.

Picking up an already comatose Dotty, I wonder whether he's going to give us the extra sheets we need, but as he leads us past a large refectory table to a spiral staircase hidden in the corner, he merely warns us to take care on the steep stairs. Hoping against hope that we're not all bunked in together, I follow the small man, carefully balancing dog and suitcase, round and up to a shadowy long narrow hall.

'Mother has already made up two beds,' he comments as he opens the first door, leaving me to wonder where the elusive mother is now. Then deciding I'm just too tired to think about it, I selfishly commandeer the first room, take note of where the bathroom is and collapse fully clothed on to my bed without bothering to turn on the light. My last thought before I drift off, is not about Noah, but to wonder whether my father and Mabel intend to share a room...

Chapter Five

I'm woken up the next morning by Dotty pawing at my face indicating her need for the bathroom. Groaning, I attempt to turn over, then suddenly realize I'm lying fully clothed on top of the covers. The events of the previous twenty-four hours come rushing back, and I sit up in panic.

Noah...

Diving into my pocket, I fumble for my mobile phone, only to discover there's no signal. Almost weeping with fear that he may have tried to call, I jump off the bed and rush over to the small narrow window. Nothing. Looking around frantically, I spy a long moth eaten settle at the bottom of the bed and drag it over to the window. Climbing on, I manage to push open the window and hold the phone up and out. Two bars. I stand, awkwardly holding out one hand, to see if I have any missed calls. Ten minutes and a dead arm later, I have to admit defeat. If Noah's tried to call, he definitely hasn't left me a message.

Hurriedly, I climb down and, barely glancing at my room, I open the door and rush back down to the Great Hall, risking life and limb by taking the spiral stairs two at a time. I have time to notice that the fire is still blazing in the hearth before crossing the room at a dead run, Dotty barking happily behind me, obviously thinking this is some new game.

Dragging open the front door, I look down again at my phone, only to see the signal come and go. I almost reach the edge of the loch before the indicator steadies at two bars. Sitting down on a large rock, I make an effort to calm myself before calling up Noah's number on speed dial.

Taking a deep breath, I tap his name. After a brief pause, it goes straight to answer phone. I sit and listen to the message, simply to hear Noah's beautiful voice, and longing cuts right down to the very core of me. God, I miss him so much. Hearing the beep, I cut the call, then try again. After five times, I have to presume he's still out of range. Sighing, I put the phone back in my pocket, knowing it will need charging soon.

Resting my chin in my hand, I watch Dotty nosing about at the edge of the water, then, realizing I have no idea what time it is, I glance down at my watch. Just after seven. No wonder there wasn't anyone around to witness my mad sprint out of the house. Although it's still only August, the morning is cool, hinting at the autumn to come. Shivering slightly, I tuck my arms under my armpits, grateful for the extra warmth of my old cardigan. All is silent apart from birdsong, and unbidden, I feel the magic of the place sweep me up again. Noah would so love it here, I muse, before remembering I might never get the opportunity to show it to him. Despairingly, I drop my head into my hands, only to jump as my phone suddenly rings. Heart beating, I look down quickly to see a number I don't recognize.

Hesitantly, I answer the call. 'I'm not going to ask where you are,' comes a matter-of-fact voice I recognize as Harry's. 'I just wanted to let you know the shit's going to hit the fan tomorrow. The *Daily Mail's* got the scoop, but the other buggers will get in on the act soon enough. Glad you're out of Dartmouth. Don't bloody come back for the next few days at least.' Then he hangs up without giving me a chance to speak.

That gives me twenty-four hours to break the news to Noah. He said he should be back in signal range by the weekend, and today's Friday. Which of course means he'll get back to civilization just in time for the party...

Dusting myself down, I call Dotty and head back to the house. As I pick my way along the uneven path, I take my first good look at our bolt hole in the daylight. Clearly in need of major refurbishment, Bloodstone Tower nevertheless radiates romantic mystery and bloodthirsty history in equal measure. In an effort to take my mind off my problems, I speculate as to why the house has been allowed to get into such disrepair. Plainly, money has to be an issue. Staring up at the old stone walls, I wonder if there are any little Buchannans to take up the mantle. After all, Hugo has to be about the same age as my father if they joined up together.

The huge front door is still open as I reach the house, and after pulling it shut behind me, I go through into the Great Hall, now much less imposing with sunlight streaming in through the windows. It's still empty, so I don't stop. I definitely need a shower, and seeing as my vague memories from last night are telling me there's only one bathroom, I decide to try and get in first. However, once I get to the top of the stairs, I can't actually remember which door is the bathroom. Frowning, I retreat into my bedroom which, in daylight, displays the same spartan furnishings as the rest of the house.

Picking Dotty up, I put her onto the high bed. She wastes no time making herself comfortable, so I leave her to it, grabbing my toiletry bag and dressing gown from my case. After discovering a clean towel on the back of a chair, I venture back out onto the landing. All is completely silent. No telltale snores coming from behind any of the doors. Bugger. I stand still and try to remember Hugo's bathroom directions from last night.

Tiptoeing down the hall, I endeavour to guess which room my father and Mabel might be in. God forbid I should open their door accidentally. Still, I'm assuming they've got Pickles in with them so that should curtail any possible funny business. Though how my father could even think of getting up to anything with all th....

My thoughts grind to a halt as I hear a noise coming from the second to last door on the right. Hesitantly, I walk towards the door in question and stop. For a second there's nothing, then I hear it again – a low keening sound as though someone's in terrible pain. Putting my ear to the wood panel, I hold my breath. The noise stops.

I don't *think* this is the bathroom. But what if someone needs help? Irresolutely, I stand at the door, undecided as to what to do next. Then, suddenly, the noise comes again. It sounds awful, like someone being tortured. Maybe I should just fetch someone – trouble is, I don't know where they all are.

In the end, I can't stand the dreadful noise any longer, and with my heart in my mouth, I quietly turn the knob and push open the door. The room is completely dark, but I can tell immediately that it's not the bathroom. Someone's bedroom then. Quietly I turn, intending to go back out into the corridor and close the door behind me, but just as I do, the keening noise comes again, and turning back round, I can vaguely see a large bed. With someone in it. Oh God, what if whoever's in there is really ill?

Cautiously I tiptoe towards the shadowy bed whispering, 'Hello, are you okay?' I'm so intent on the indistinct lump under the covers, that I completely miss the chamber pot sitting on the floor next to the side of the bed. 'Hello,' I whisper a little more loudly. I take one last hesitant step, only to have my bare foot land directly in the pot. Which is not empty. I give a small, stifled scream and try to lift out my foot, inadvertently stubbing my big toe in the process and kicking the pot over which breaks against the edge of the bed with a loud crack, spilling its wet contents onto the floor. Moaning softly, I start to clutch at my toe before remembering what it's been standing in. Unfortunately, the momentum has me toppling helplessly towards the bed and its occupant. After flailing for a heart stopping couple of seconds, I land with a small woomph directly onto the lump…

…Which sits up screaming as if all the hounds of hell are after her. Yes, despite the murkiness, I can tell it's a her. 'Please – please, it's okay,' I moan holding out my hand in a placatory gesture while hopping up and down on one foot (well you try it). 'I just thought you needed help,' (it sounded much more plausible when I was lurking outside her door). When she fails to stop screaming, I hurriedly turn and hobble back towards the landing, all the while shouting backwards, 'It's okay, it's okay, I'm so sorry, please forgive me, I'm so so sorry.'

'What the bollocking hell is going on?' I cringe with further embarrassment as my father throws open the door to my left and shouts loud enough to wake anyone else who by some miracle has so far managed to sleep through the ruckus. (I'm not too embarrassed to make a mental note of which room he's in though…) Both Pickles and Dotty add to the racket from behind their respective bedroom doors and finally Hugo Buchannan emerges with a look of complete astonishment on his face.

'I'm so sorry,' I babble again waving towards what is obviously his mother's room, 'I didn't realize she was just snoring.' He stares back at me hopping up and down for a second, then, shaking his head, rushes into the darkened room, shouting, 'It's alright, Mother.'

A couple of seconds later, Kit and Freddy emerge out of their respective rooms, and I can't help but think, almost hysterically, 'Oh goody, now we can have a party.'

'Why are you hopping up and down?' Freddy gets in just before the door to Hugo's mother's room slams shut. I hold out my throbbing foot which Freddy bends down to peer at. 'I accidently kicked over the chamber pot,' I say, causing him to back up sharply as though the liquid contaminating my foot is likely to turn airborne at any second.

'What the bloody hell were you doing in there?' thunders my father.

'Is that Hugo's mother making that terrible noise?' Kit asks.

'What on earth did you do to her?' Freddy demands.

'I thought she was having a heart attack,' I desperately explain.

The howling noise coming from my bedroom reaches epic proportions. Dotty.

Finally, in desperation, I shout, 'QUIET,' then in the ensuing silence, I look at each of my friends in turn before saying softly, 'It's going to be in the *Daily Mail* tomorrow.'

As twilight fell on the stark landscape, the director finally called out, 'It's a wrap,' prompting a smatter of relieved applause. The heat throughout the day had been intense, fraying tempers and fuelling petty irritations. After being helped out of his custom-made space suit, Noah pulled on a pair of shorts and headed over to the generated air-conditioned bliss of the communal tent for the last time. Tomorrow they would be heading back down to the coast, and he'd finally get to speak to Tory. Helping himself to a large glass of water, he wiped the sweat from his forehead with a towel, grateful that he no longer had to avoid messing up the carefully applied make-up.

It had been a long exhausting few days, and as he stood at the entrance to the tent and watched the last of the sun's rays turn the harsh mountains into a fiery orange, Noah didn't think he'd ever been so happy to finish a location shoot. If he could, he'd leave immediately, but tonight they were having a get-together before the cast and crew split up - some moving on to Ireland, the rest heading back to the States. He knew he'd be expected to attend the party, despite his distinct lack of enthusiasm. Sighing, he quickly poured the rest of the water over his head, and made his way towards his own tent, intending to grab a quick shower while the water was still warm. Then, with any luck, he'd manage a short rest before the revelry started.

It was fully dark by the time Noah came out of his tent. Although the festivities had started a couple of hours ago, he'd avoided joining the party too early, knowing it was likely to go on until the early hours of the morning. Wearing shorts and a simple white t-shirt, Noah was completely unaware of the hungry looks directed towards him from both men and women alike as he walked over to the makeshift bar to grab a beer. Taking a long swig, he strolled over to Laurel standing near to the large barbeque. The delicious smell of roasting meat coming from the grill made his stomach clench in anticipation as he suddenly realized he hadn't eaten since breakfast.

'God, I could eat a horse,' she groaned, echoing his thoughts exactly. 'I'm not moving from here until the first burger's ready – and trust me, it has my name on it.'

The sound of laughter echoed from a large group standing a few yards away, obviously more interested in drinking than eating, which suited Noah just fine.

'You hoping to get a bit of quality time with Tory before we kick off again? Especially given the fact that we've got all of three days before we need to show up.' Laurel's smile softened the sarcasm, and her voice held a slightly sympathetic tone. Noah grimaced in response. 'I'm hoping so,' he said with a sigh, 'But I've not managed to speak with her since we arrived in Tenerife, so I've no idea what her plans are.'

'I don't think you have to worry about any plans she's made,' the actress responded as she helped herself to a burger. 'She'll drop whatever she's doing to see you, I'm sure.'

Noah nodded absently, taking the next beef pattie from the tray. A queue was beginning to form behind him as people realized the food was ready, and he didn't want to discuss his love life in front of the people he worked with. His nagging worry about Tory was still there. This was probably the longest they'd gone without speaking since they started dating.

Moving away from the barbeque with his spoils, he looked around for somewhere a little less noisy, eventually spotting an abandoned deckchair positioned to make the most of the spectacular views of the valley and mountains beyond. Seating himself with a sigh, Noah took another long draught of his beer before placing the bottle on the stony ground next to him. There was just enough light cast by the camp to see by, and the loud raucous laughter was pleasantly muted. He knew he'd have to go back and mingle eventually, but for a little while, he was determined to enjoy the peace and quiet.

The valley and mountains in front of him were simply dark outlines, and as he dug into his burger, he absently tried to make out the shapes in the blackness. If he closed his eyes slightly, he could just make out sections of the potholed road winding round the valley and up the mountains. He definitely wasn't looking forward to the ride back to the coast.

Suddenly, he saw two lights flashing, quickly, then gone. For a couple of seconds, he thought he might be seeing things, then he saw them again. Frowning he studied their intermittent blinking, wondering what the hell they were. Then he realized. They were the headlights of a car. Someone was coming up the mountain. Bloody hell, they were taking a bit of a risk in the dark, so it had to be important.

As Noah sat and watched the lights get larger, he felt his gut clench. The burger felt like a lump of lead in his stomach, and suddenly feeling slightly sick, he put the half-empty plate on the ground. After another five minutes or so, he could finally hear the car engine, slowly getting louder as the vehicle approached their camp. Others were beginning to realize they had company, and some were wandering curiously down to the large flat area that served as a makeshift car park. Noah stayed where he was, watching the scene from the shadows. He could just see the side of the car park behind the communal tent, and, in the light shed from the large marquee, he finally glimpsed the car approach. It was battered and dirty with faint writing on the side. Obviously, a taxi. Heart hammering, he finally stood up just as the back door opened. Then he was running.

A few minutes later he rounded the tent and skidded to a halt in front of the rumpled portly form of his agent. Staring at Tim's tense sombre features, Noah turned towards the interested onlookers and took a deep breath, trying to relax his racing heart.

'Tim,' he finally said mildly as though he'd been expecting to see his agent in the middle of nowhere at such a late hour. 'Great to see you, come and have a drink.' He put his arm companionably around the corpulent man's shoulders and made as if to guide him towards the festivities. It had the desired effect. Seeing nothing of interest happening, their spectators waved a casual greeting and turned to head back up the hill. Once they were out of earshot, Noah stopped and turned to face his agent.

'What?' he said tersely, his worry making his voice clipped and abrupt. 'Has something happened to Tory?'

Tim took a deep breath before answering. Underneath his anxious exterior, there seemed to be an almost edgy, nervous excitement to his body language. 'We've got a problem, Noah, and it's a whopper.'

Chapter Six

Breakfast is a fairly subdued affair. Mrs. Buchannan has sent her apologies, with Hugo saying hastily that his mother has suffered no ill effects from my early morning visit but prefers to keep herself to herself and avoid polite company whenever possible.

'Especially when supposed polite company starts off by scaring the living daylights out of her,' murmurs Freddy behind his teacup. I take the moral high ground by refusing to rise to the bait. However, privately I can't help but think that if this house has been featured on *Britain's Most Haunted*, it was likely old Mrs. Buchannan who was doing the honours.

We are seated at the refectory table in the Great Hall, and our breakfast orders are taken by a plump lady of indeterminate age called Aileen who is evidently Hugo's "woman who does" as he jokingly referred to her. I'm reluctant to ask exactly what she "does" aside from breakfasts, partly because I'm not actually sure I want to know, but mostly because I can't understand a word she says. Her greeting when we first arrived for breakfast sounded something like, 'Awrite, guid mornin, nice tae meit ye.' After she took our order, she cheerily announced, 'A hae tae gang, a'll be reit back,' and on returning with the breakfast tray, 'Haur ye gae.' Fortunately, she didn't appear to be expecting a response at any time during the whole procedure.

My father doesn't appear to have lost his appetite due to our bit of a problem, and as I watch him take his third potato scone and fourth helping of black pudding, I really wish I have his resilience. I look down at my porridge and give it an experimental stir. My stomach feels as though it's in knots, and I'm not sure I can eat anything. Forcing down a small spoonful out of politeness, I look around the table to see that everybody else's appetite seems to be holding up just fine. Kit is busy tucking into yoghurt, fruit, tea and toast, while Mabel's plate is piled nearly as high as my father's. Freddy's the only one picking listlessly at his plate of sausage, bacon and eggs which is why Dotty has chosen to do her begging routine next to his seat. She can spot the weakest link from twenty paces.

Suddenly, the phone rings. Sadly, we all actually go to check our mobiles, only to realize it's a land line. Hugo excuses himself quickly and, picking up the handset, takes it into what I'm assuming is the kitchen, although I haven't had the chance to explore yet. A few minutes later, he comes back into the Great Hall, and his face is serious. Everyone else is busy eating, so I think I'm the only one who sees him shake his head slightly at my father. Looking between the two of them, I can sense the slight tension. What the hell is going on? I'm about to open my mouth to demand some kind of explanation, when suddenly, Mabel decides to speak.

'Do you have balls, Mr. Buchannan?' she says loudly as Hugo sits back down to the table.

We all stare at her in silence as our host responds hesitantly, 'Call me Hugo, please.' He's clearly unsure what to say next, which makes six of us.

'I mean to say, have you held any here in Bloodstone Tower?' Mabel's idea of small talk definitely leaves a lot to be desired, I'm beginning to think she and my father make the perfect couple. Looking at our slightly bemused faces, she hurriedly continues, clearly flustered but determined to make polite conversation. 'Or perhaps you've attended them elsewhere. Charles has told me so many wonderful stories about the balls he's attended over the years, along with so many wonderful people, but strangely he's never mentioned you.' All our eyes turn towards Hugo to see what his response is likely to be in light of the fact that my father's lady friend has just indicated that the Admiral has never deemed our host worth mentioning.

'Bloody hell, Mabel,' my father jumps in tetchily before Hugo can respond, causing everyone's eyes to swing to him. 'Give it a rest. You can be such a gatling gob at times.' Then he stands up, pushes back his chair, and stomps off outside, calling to Pickles as he goes. I look towards Mabel and can see her chin wobbling slightly.

'Don't pay any attention to him,' I tell her softly as she gets up to leave the table. 'He's just worried, and you know how rude he gets when he's worried.'

I ignore Freddy mouthing, 'What's a gatling gob?' from behind Mabel's back and look towards Hugo to see if he's taken offence. To my relief, he doesn't look as though he's planning to throw us out on our ears. I really want to ask him what the head shaking was all about, but before I can say anything further, he excuses himself and hurries after my father. Sighing, I take another mouthful of my now stone-cold porridge which is starting to resemble wallpaper paste.

'So, peeps, what shall we do today?' Freddy trills in a strained attempt to turn our enforced isolation into something out of a *Famous Five* adventure.

'Well, I don't know about you two, but I'm intending to spend the next twenty-four hours wherever I can get a signal for my phone.' As Freddy begins to frown, I add quietly, 'I have to keep trying Noah.'

'Well, the weather's lovely,' Kit says, her voice muffled as she pops the last slice of melon into her mouth. 'We can take a picnic, you know, with hard boiled eggs and lashings of ginger beer...' She says the last bit with a wink towards Freddy, and I have to smile. 'You shouldn't be on your own,' she continues more seriously. 'That's why we're here.' Giving in, I smile gratefully at them both.

'I wonder if they've got any potted meat?' muses Freddy, enthusiastically pushing his chair back and heading towards the kitchen. 'I'll go and ask Aileen.'

'Good luck with that,' I say to his retreating back. Still hoping for leftovers, Dotty immediately trots after him, and I shake my head ruefully. I could call her back, but she's likely to throw a deaf ear if I do. Where food's concerned, obedience doesn't come in to it, and the greedy madam will do anything for a sausage. As she follows him into the kitchen, barking happily, I hear Aileen say, 'Haud yer wheesht.' No idea if she's talking to Freddy or my canine opportunist.

Leaving Kit and Freddy to keep an eye on her and sort out our very own fifties inspired, retro *Famous Five* picnic, I grab my phone off its charge and head out in search of my father and Hugo.

Following the sound of voices, I walk towards the loch and continue down a path running alongside it. As the voices get louder, I slow down instinctively.

'It's no good, Scotty, if they won't get involved, I'm just going to have to face the music.' It takes me a couple of seconds to realize that my father's talking to Hugo and not the balding engineer from the Starship Enterprise, although I'm assuming the nickname similarly refers to his heritage. I can't quite make out Hugo's response, and in my effort to get closer, I give away the fact that I'm lurking in the bushes as Pickles catches my scent and begins wagging his tail in welcome.

'Stop arsing about, Victory.' My father's voice sounds

frighteningly weary, and suddenly scared, I swallow a sharp retort and continue the last few yards to a small wooden landing poking out into the loch. The two men are seated side by side on a rickety bench.

'What's going on, Dad?' I ask flatly, positioning myself squarely in front of them. 'There's so much more to this than you're letting on. Why have we come all the way up here – no offence Hugo – when we could have hidden out equally well somewhere like Dartmoor, just a few bloody miles away from home?'

 'That's exactly what they'd be expecting.'

'Bullshit,' I snap, finally at the end of my tether with all the lying and subterfuge. 'This is my life, Dad. Tell me what this is all about – *really* all about.' My father blinks as my voice reaches a crescendo. 'Would you like to tell the rest of bollocking Scotland too?' he returns irritably.

'She's definitely your daughter,' butts in Hugo with a slight chuckle. 'Did she ever think of joining up?' I glare back at him. If he's attempting to diffuse the situation, he's not doing a very good job.

My father evidently thinks so too. 'She'd have done a better bloody job than you, Scotty. You were always all fart and no shit.'

'You may well be right, Charlie, but if you'd have been more fart and less shit, we might not be in this mess.'

'Dad, you out on the landing?' A loud unidentified male voice abruptly interrupts the rapidly escalating argument, and for a second, I'm relieved, until I look down at Hugo's horrified face and realize whoever the voice belongs to, he's definitely not part of the plan.

The owner of the voice appears a few seconds later, and I stare at him with my mouth open.

'This is my son, Jason,' Hugo says, making a concerted effort not to show that his offspring is the very last person he expected to see. 'Jason, I don't believe you've met my old friend Charles Shackleford and his daughter, Victory.'

'Call me Tory,' I interject a little faintly. It has to be said that Jason looks absolutely nothing like his father. Dressed in a t-shirt and jeans that do little to hide what is obviously six feet of solid muscle, he is absolutely gorgeous. His hair is perhaps the only thing he's inherited from his father, but instead of a bright ginger it's a thick burnished chestnut. His skin is bronzed, speaking of too much time spent in the sun, contrasting with eyes the colour of polished silver. And right now, those eyes are looking at me as though he has a bad smell under his nose.

'*Admiral* Charles Shackleford?' is all he says as his eyes dismiss me and settle back on his father.

'Yes, well, of course you've heard of him.' Hugo is visibly flustered, and I frown, but before I can speak, Hugo turns to us and continues, 'Jason's in the Royal Navy too. He's just been promoted after spending the last three years in Hawaii.' Then back to his son. 'I wasn't expecting you to be back so soon.'

'Clearly,' is the flat answer. I'm beginning to think Mr. Gorgeous may well turn out to be a complete and utter knob.

'Dad, I think you and I need to talk privately,' he continues in the same flat monotone voice before turning away and striding back down the path without waiting to see if his father is following.

Hugo shakes his head glumly at both of us as he gets up. 'Bollocks. I wasn't expecting Jason to be back before next week. Might cause a bit of a problem.' As I watch his small figure hasten up the path, I sit down in his vacated seat with a small, defeated sigh. I get the feeling he and my father might well refer to the outbreak of World War III as a bit of a problem...

For the next few minutes, we sit silently, staring out over the loch. The breeze has turned the previously calm water into small choppy waves splashing noisily up against the small landing. I glance down at my mobile phone to check it has a signal. 'Are you ever going to tell me what happened, Dad?' I ask in a small voice. 'You've told me practically nothing so far, and what you have said is a complete cock and bull story, don't even bother to deny it. Just tell me if you killed that man. Are you truly a murderer, or are you some kind of scapegoat?'

After a small silence, he exhales noisily. 'I've killed men in my time, Victory,' he says after a moment, 'But never in cold-blooded murder. I can't tell you what happened. You'll just have to trust me.'

'Even if it loses me the man I love?' I ask quietly.

He closes his eyes to avoid looking at me. 'Noah's a good chap,' he mumbles finally. 'If he truly loves you, he won't walk away.'

I jump up and stalk to the edge of the loch in an effort to stem the frustrated anger mounting inside me that my father could spout such meaningless drivel to *me* of all people. Does he think me completely stupid - even he doesn't believe that twaddle for one bloody second. 'I won't let him choose me over his career,' I say finally through gritted teeth. 'You know that. Stop treating me like a child.' Then, without looking back at him, 'I have to stay outside, Dad. I can't get a signal inside the house.' He doesn't respond, and neither does he move, so I take a deep breath and continue in a whisper, 'I need some time on my own. Please can you just go away?'

The day has crawled by. It's now nearly six o'clock, and I've been sitting on the landing for nearly eight hours, trying Noah's mobile phone every twenty minutes. Kit and Freddy have finally left me to it, and Dotty, whose loyalty in the face of potential starvation is sketchy at best, has abandoned me in favour of her new best friend, Aileen. Both Kit and Freddy have done their best throughout the day to keep me cheerful, putting together a banquet worthy of Enid Blyton at her most ravenous. To be fair, it's actually been quite nice, but as the hours have worn on, my anxiety has become harder and harder to ignore. Neither of my friends got to bump into the gorgeous knob before exiting the house, so I didn't enlighten them, preferring to witness firsthand their impressions over dinner. I haven't seen my father again since this morning either, but that's okay. I think we're better off ignoring each other at the moment.

The wind's beginning to get up, and the summer sun, never that warm in Scotland, is giving way to an early evening autumnesque chill. I know I can't sit here much longer. My back's aching, and my bottom's gone completely numb. I try Noah's mobile one last time, then get to my feet to go inside and wash up before dinner.

The fire in the Great Hall is blazing merrily, which is very welcome in the face of the escalating blustery weather outside. Kit and Freddy are sitting together playing cards, my traitorous mutt sandwiched between them snoring. As I look around the lofty room, taking in the ancient tapestries, musty and discoloured from hanging so long, I can't help but reflect just what I could do with a few metres of tartan and a generous budget. Freddy waves me over to join them, but not in the mood for games, I simply wave back and wander through into the kitchen, up to now uncharted territory.

An archway from the Great Hall leads to a narrow low-ceilinged passageway before opening up into what appears to have been a kitchen since the tower was built, probably sometime in the fifteenth century. The ceiling is vaulted, and the units look as though they might have been top of the range in the Middle Ages. I stand at the entrance, reluctant to disturb Aileen as she bustles around what is clearly her domain, putting the finishing touches to our evening meal. I can't tell what she's cooking, but whatever it is smells delicious. After a minute or so, she turns and spots me lurking in the doorway.

'Ah, guid eenin,' she beams, wiping her hands on a tea towel. 'Hou's aw wi ye?' Having no idea what she's talking about, I take a cue from her manner and smile hesitantly back before moving further into the room. 'Dinner smells heavenly,' I say with a deep appreciative sniff.

'Thenk ye,' is her answer, for once blessedly comprehensible, and I grin back at her, all the while bobbing my head up and down like a nodding dog. I'm just about to take the plunge and ask her what she's cooking, when suddenly a black streak shoots through an open window followed a couple of seconds later by a frenziedly barking Pickles who appears to have morphed into Super Spaniel as he literally flies through the window and lands with a huge splash in the washing up bowl.

Finding herself abruptly drenched with doggy scented soap suds, Aileen shrieks and covers her head with her apron.

By the time the shock of his sudden bath has worn off, the black cat is long gone, a simple fact that Pickles grasps not at all, and after a couple of stunned seconds, he scrambles out of the sink, knocking over a large pan of partially peeled potatoes resting on the draining board. Barking with renewed excitement, he skates across the kitchen on a rolling sea of spuds as Aileen yells, 'Och ye scunner, watch ma tatties,' before disappearing into the passageway leaving a muddy wet trail behind him.

We stand wordlessly for a couple of stunned seconds until the silence is broken by my father huffing and puffing through the kitchen door.

'You seen Pickles?' he breathes, hanging onto the door handle. 'He spotted a damn cat and suddenly decides he's the canine equivalent of Usain Bolt. Don't know who the hell the bloody flea-bitten thing belongs to, but I saw 'em coming this way.' Aileen points mutely towards the passageway, just as the ear-splitting sound of howling and barking, together with a sudden crash, reverberates into the kitchen. The deafening racket puts an end to my trance, and with an apologetic grimace towards Aileen, I dash out of the kitchen towards the pandemonium coming from the Great Hall.

As I skid into the room, my heart hits my feet as I take in the scene before me. The cat is hanging for dear life at the top of a pair of moth-eaten curtains which are ripping in slow motion as a result of Pickles and Dotty hanging enthusiastically on the bottom. The other end of each dog is being held by Kit and Freddy as they vainly try to get the bloodthirsty twosome to let go. 'What a complete horlicks,' my father mutters as he appears beside me. 'PICKLES.' He changes volume with no warning, and for a brief second, I think I've gone deaf, then he strides towards the chaos yelling, 'GET DOWN OFF THAT BOLLOCKING CURTAIN OR YOU'RE GOING TO BE RELEGATED TO THE GARAGE FOR THE REST OF YOUR BLOODY NATURAL.'

Now I'm assuming Pickles is not actually able to understand English, but it only takes one glance back at his master to tell him he's in big trouble. He immediately lets go of the material, and Freddy promptly goes flying back onto the unforgiving flagstone floor with Pickles on top of him. Simultaneously, Kit lets go of Dotty in surprise and without the spaniel's weight to hold it down, the curtain material springs upwards with the little dog still holding on by her teeth. I gasp but know I'm too far away to save her if she falls. Luckily, Kit has it under control, and with an agile leap, she manages to grab hold of Dotty, who unfortunately is completely unappreciative of her brush with potential death and refuses to let go of the curtain. With a loud rending sound, the fragile material parts completely and lands squarely on Kit's head covering her like a shroud.

'What the hell is going on?' The curt voice is not loud but nevertheless cuts through the pandemonium like a knife through butter, and we all instantly look in the direction of the clipped tones. Shit, it's the knob, and call me intuitive, but he doesn't look happy.

For a couple of seconds, the only sounds are Kit's muffled profanities as she struggles to get the curtain off her head, then suddenly, a high-pitched scream splits the air. We all turn towards the sound in time to see old Mrs. Buchannan framed by the front door with her hand clutching her heart.

'It's the Lady, has she come to take me o'or th'other side then?' she wails in a warbling voice before falling in a dead faint at our feet.

I'm beginning to think Hugo's mother might not actually survive if we stay more than a few days.

I think I can safely say that dinner is not turning out to be the lighthearted happy affair we might all have hoped for. Mrs. Buchannan is once again absent after being put to bed for the second time in one day. I've apologized profusely, promising to replace the damaged curtains at the earliest opportunity, but while Hugo seems inclined to accept my humble apology, waving away the incident by saying his mother has always had a penchant for theatrics, his son is determined not to let us off so lightly. Consequently, Pickles and Dotty have been relegated to our respective bedrooms where an occasional mournful bark can be heard from upstairs. Spike the cat, who by the look of him, has been here nearly as long as the Tower, is enjoying the spoils of victory – a bag of purring contented bones warming by the fire.

Conversation started out stilted and has now deteriorated into excruciating silence. Jason Buchannan, unlike the rest of us, has obviously dressed for dinner and, much as it pains me to admit it, looks completely yummy in white shirt and chinos. I can't help but notice (well there isn't a lot else going on) that his hair is a burnished copper in the lamplight. It's just a shame he looks as though he's been sucking a lemon. As the silence becomes unbearable, I begin racking my brains for something to say. Unfortunately, Mabel gets there first.

'Is it a sort of legend, this err Lady?' she asks him timidly, 'You know, like the woman in that film with Harry Potter in it?' Freddy titters nervously, but the knob just looks over at the elderly matron, distaste in every line as he stares at her without answering.

Outraged at his rudeness, I open my mouth to give him the dressing down he deserves, when unexpectedly Kit jumps in. 'Is everyone this inhospitable in Scotland, or is it just you?' I glance over at my best friend in astonishment. Although her voice is quite calm, her face is flushed, and I can tell she's furious. This is so not like my Kitty Kat.

The knob stares back at her for a couple of seconds, then inclines his head before saying stiffly to an embarrassed Mabel, 'I apologize if I was rude, ma'am. My only defence is my fatigue. It has been a very long day. I think perhaps my father might be better placed to answer your question.' Hurriedly, Hugo takes up the story of Bloodstone Tower's ghost, clearly eager to brush over the awkwardness.

Although the Tower actually got its name from the colour of the stone, rather than its bloody history, there were nevertheless enough macabre goings on to have provided a whole series of *Britain's Most Haunted*. Mrs. Buchannan's Lady apparently refers to a woman who was imprisoned in the attic of the Tower many centuries ago and starved to death. Although, it's not quite clear what she did to merit such a horrible fate, her kinsmen supposedly tried valiantly to rescue her, but were themselves caught, murdered and their bodies thrown from a top storey window. Evidently, their blood even now stains the floorboards in the attic, and the Lady's anguished cries can still be heard echoing around the Tower on certain days of the year. I stifle the urge to ask which days, hopeful that we'll be gone before she decides to show herself for real...

Although undoubtedly interesting, Hugo's tale of murder and mayhem does little to lighten the frosty atmosphere, and I excuse myself as soon as we're finished, going up to fetch Dotty and escape outside where the wind has finally died down. Unfortunately, once outside in the dusk of early evening, I very quickly realize that we are providing a three-course banquet for the bloody midges, and after Dotty sits down and refuses to go any further, repeatedly shaking her head and snapping at the tiny, almost invisible bugs, I give up and retreat back into the Great Hall.

Kit, Freddy and Mabel are playing cards by the fire. Jason is seated at a desk in the far corner writing something in what appears from this distance to be some kind of journal. Probably his very own book of evil spells. I wonder where he's hidden his cauldron. There is no sign of Hugo or my father. Spike too has disappeared off to indulge in whatever feline sins of the night appeal to balding emaciated cats, so I let Dotty off the lead and go to join my friends.

It's going to be a long night.

It's nearly midnight, and I'm back outside for the second time this evening with my mobile phone plastered to my ear – I'm beginning to think I might need it surgically removed by the time I finally get hold of Noah. Dotty and I are wandering along the side of the loch. The strange half light is casting fantastical purple shadows over the darkened landscape, creating a world more suited to Middle Earth. The midges have gone back to wherever midges live when they're not eating people alive – apparently, it's only at dusk they're a problem. As we pick our way slowly along the shoreline, I wonder how long we're actually going to be able to stay at Bloodstone Tower. Jason Buchannan is clearly suspicious of our motives, which makes me think he knows something already. But even if he doesn't, once he hears the news tomorrow, our bags could well be out on the drive quicker than you can say, 'guilty milord.' I get the feeling that Hugo doesn't really run the estate anymore, but I know he's involved in this mess somewhere and most definitely doesn't want his poker-faced son to know about it.

Deep in thought, I step down to the small beach and idly pick up pebbles to throw into the water. If Jason does throw us out, I don't care what Dad thinks, I'm going back to Dartmouth and sod the press. It's truly beautiful up here, but if I'm going to have to lick my wounds somewhere, I'd rather it be home. With that decision made, I finally feel a measure of peace - which promptly shatters as my phone rings, the trilling shockingly loud in the quiet.

Finally. At last.

It's Noah.

Chapter Seven

Forty years ago...

The evening was sultry and humid, the heat still up in the mid-nineties. Lieutenants Charles Shackleford and Hugo Buchannan had been assigned to accompany a lowly sub lieutenant on a sightseeing tour of Bangkok. This was unusual for several reasons, the chief of which was that a serving sub lieutenant would be very unlikely to be given a sightseeing tour of anything except maybe the inside of his superior officer's broom cupboard. But this particular sub lieutenant was not all he seemed. He had "connections", except that no-one really knew exactly what they were. There was of course a lot of onboard conjecture and speculation. However, the real truth remained irritatingly elusive, and Sub Lieutenant John Day remained plain old Sub Lieutenant John Day - or Doris as he became known on board, in true Royal Naval tradition of why give someone a proper name when a nickname will do. (In this case alluding to Doris Day, the thinking man's pin up back in the sixties).

So, getting back to Lieutenant Shackleford's orders, which came straight from the top. 'Sub Lieutenant Day would like to learn about Thai culture. You, Lieutenant Buchannan and Able Seaman Noon will accompany him on a run ashore to Bangkok, show him the sights, take him round a few Buddhist temples and stuff. I want him back on board no later than twenty-three hundred hours. Make sure you keep an eye on things Shackleford – and that means making sure that nothing bad happens to our

Doris, or make no mistake, your balls are likely to end up round your neck.'

Lieutenant Shackleford didn't think that learning about Thai culture extended to obtaining a working knowledge of the capital's brothels; however, Doris had bribed their guide, and within half an hour, here they were, bang smack in the middle of Bangkok's red-light district. Of course, it didn't actually say brothel over the door. The sign said "Ap Ob Nuat", which their guide Kulap assured Charlie was Thai for "Steamy Hot Shower Massage."

The problem was, Doris had been enjoying his steamy hot shower massage for the last forty-five minutes, and they were running out of time. Even their guide was starting to look a bit agitated, and, as more of the locals began to show interest in the three "farang", he kept looking towards the back door as if gauging how long it was likely to take him to leg it there if he needed to do a runner. Charlie felt the sweat begin to run down his back and not totally from the humidity. His captain was going to have his balls for this.

'What the bloody hell's taking so long?' he hissed to Hugo. 'You think one of us should go up to have a shufti?' Both officers turned in unison towards the third member of their party. Completely oblivious to the tensions around the table, Jimmy Noon was busy writing a letter to his fiancée. As the silence finally penetrated his literary absorption, the small man looked up, surprise and wariness chasing themselves across his face when he realized his companions were staring at him.

'Mr. Noon, I'd like you to take a look upstairs and see what the bloody hell Dori..., I mean Subby Day, is doing. When you find him, please inform him that we need to get our arses back to the ship, pronto.'

Jimmy opened his mouth to protest, then closed it again with a sigh. Why else had he been brought along if not to do any necessary dirty work? Folding up his letter, he tucked it into his jacket pocket and stood up, noting as he did so, that every eye in the house was suddenly on him, causing a vague uneasiness to prickle down his spine.

'Where should I look, Sir?' Jimmy whispered, stalling for time.

'Just start at the first door and look behind each one until you find him. Simple.'

'But what if there's someone else behind one of the doors, you know, someone other than Dori..., Sub Lieutenant Day?'

'Always allow for a self-adjusting cock up Mr. Noon, carry on.' Lieutenant Shackleford's voice was relatively mild but made it clear that any refusal to implement the proposed recce would be considered insubordination.

Jimmy nodded his understanding and, stepping round their table, headed in what he hoped was a nonchalant manner towards the stairs. If anyone stopped him, he could say he was looking for the heads. The steps up to the first floor were rickety to say the least. Their guide certainly hadn't brought them to the classiest of Bangkok's "steamy hot shower massage" establishments; the emphasis here was not so much steamy as sweaty. As he continued casually up towards the first-floor landing, Jimmy could feel hostile eyes boring into the back of his head, and he resisted the urge to bolt for the upstairs hallway.

After what seemed like hours but was probably less than two minutes, he finally arrived at the beginning of a long dim corridor. He took a deep breath. 'Lieutenant Day?' he murmured, knocking at the first door, with his ear plastered to the ancient wood.

Nothing.

Softly he opened the door and peeked into the room. Empty.

He continued down the passageway, heart beating ridiculously fast. 'For God's sake, it's only a frigging knocking shop,' he told himself sternly, 'get a bloody backbone, Jimbo.'

The next room was occupied by someone of Asian persuasion if the groaning gobbledygook was anything to go by. Two more rooms proved empty, which left just one more, right at the very end.

By this time, Jimmy was beginning to get a bit peed off. Why should bloody Doris Day be allowed to get his rocks off while the rest of them sat twiddling their thumbs downstairs? Who the hell was this chap? Pausing finally in front of the last door, Jimmy coughed loudly in the hope of alerting Doris that he was there. Now it seemed certain he had the correct room, he was struggling to avoid the mental picture of his superior's skinny backside bobbing up and down in time with his dangly bits. If he was forced to view the reality, it could potentially scar him for life. When the cough failed to elicit any sound whatsoever, Jimmy knocked as hard as he could and, after a short pause, followed it with, 'Sub Lieutenant Day, are you there, Sir? It's Able Seaman Noon.'

Jimmy briefly thought he heard a short scuffle, but then there was silence again. 'SUB LIEUTENANT DAY ARE YOU THERE, SIR?' This time Jimmy held nothing back and was pretty certain that if Doris was in there, he would have heard him. In fact, it was possible the whole of Bangkok's red-light district also heard him, which is why a few seconds later Charles Shackleford appeared at the top of the stairs hissing, 'You jabbering idiot, Noon, you looking to alert the whole bloody neighbourhood?'

'I don't think he's in there, S…,' Jimmy started to say, only to stop short when the door was suddenly flung open by a raven-haired beauty dressed in nothing but a tiny satin robe. Startled, Jimmy stared at the vision in front of him, all thoughts of Emily vanishing as quick as you could say, 'I'll have a quick one.' With a sultry smile, the woman pulled him through the open doorway, and after a small squeak and a panicked look back towards his superior, Jimmy found himself on the other side of the door.

Jimmy just had time to register a large bed which was definitely occupied, before finding himself fending off small hands that seemed to be everywhere at once. 'I don't, I mean I'm not, it's just, I haven't got, really you shouldn't...' The problem was, he was fast beginning to forget exactly why she shouldn't, and with a groan muffled by cherry red lips, Jimmy surrendered himself to the nimble expert fingers now busy delving down the front of his trousers. Leaning forward he sought to return the favour and eagerly parted her robe, only to be shocked back to sudden awareness when his roaming fingers found a lot more than he'd bargained for.

For a second he froze, while his fingers, seemingly with a life of their own, continued their incredulous groping as if they believed he'd somehow been mistaken. However, as the object of his fondling began to rise to the occasion, he finally came to his senses and, snatching the offending digits away, yelled in a voice loud enough to wake the dead, 'Bloody hell, it's a man.'

The shadowed lump in the bed bolted upright in response to Jimmy's panicked shout, and at the same time Charles Shackleford burst into the room behind him. Loud footsteps pounding up the stairs indicated that at least one more person was headed their way, and as Hugo Buchannan erupted into the room, there was a short silence as the three men stared at each other, then looked over to the bed.

Glancing down at his partner's equipment, Doris moaned in horrified disbelief and began hurriedly trying to extract himself from the sheets.

More footsteps running up the stairs galvanized the three men into action. 'Doris, you bloody dickhead,' muttered Charlie appropriately as he ran over to the bed to help yank off the tangled sheets, 'How the bloody hell did you get this far without realizing it was a bloke?' Then, spotting Doris's abandoned clothing on a chair, he threw them towards the bed. 'For God's sake put some bollocking trousers on.'

Two seconds later, Kulap arrived at the scene, and, after summing up the whole situation with a quick glance, promptly turned to bolt, only to be yanked back as Hugo seized hold of his jacket.

'Not so quick, sunshine. You got us into this mess, you can get us out of it.' Then pushing their hapless guide back into the corridor, he waved at the other three to follow him. 'I not know this kathoey massage place, I not know, I swear,' Kulap moaned as Hugo, who had no idea what their terrified guide was on about, simply propelled him towards the staircase.

The two kathoeys or ladyboys, who'd remained silent up to now, suddenly realized that any possibility of them adding a few "extras" to the sum already handed over were quickly disappearing, and roused themselves to start screeching in rapid ear-splitting Thai.

'What a bloody cake and arse party,' yelled Charlie as they hurried down the passageway heading for the stairs, only to come face to face with a dozen menacing figures half way down, completely blocking their escape. This time there was no mistaking the gender, or the intent, as they brandished nasty looking clubs.

Charlie and Hugo glanced towards each other, realizing for the first time that they'd be lucky if they escaped with their lives intact, let alone their tackle. Kulap stood shivering and whimpering about kathoeys, while Doris kept muttering, 'This can't be happening,' over and over again. Jimmy simply stood behind the three officers, white faced and silent.

'We'll just have to charge through them, take them by surprise,' Charlie murmured softly to Hugo. 'It's our only chance.' The red-haired Scot nodded tensely, grasping the back of Kulap's jacket in a vice as Charlie turned round to the other two. 'Follow our lead,' he whispered tersely before turning back to Hugo. 'On three,' he said softly without taking his eyes off the mob slowly ascending the stairs. 'Let's give 'em the banshee treatment.'

'One, two, THREE.' Launching themselves down the stairs screaming like banshees with piles, they charged straight into the astonished rabble, knocking them for six and scoring a strike as they all bounced down the stairs to land in a big heap at the bottom. Without waiting to see if they'd done any damage, Charlie dragged Jimmy and Doris up by their collars and pushed them in the direction of the door. Then, turning back to the melee, he pulled Hugo and Kulap from the now groaning pile of bodies. As the three of them reached the exit, they turned back briefly to watch the disorientated men climb to their feet. Luckily, all the thugs were alive and kicking, so breathing a sigh of relief, Charlie turned back to his companions and shoved them out of the door.

Chapter Eight

Noah sat in the back of the taxi as it made its way precariously down the dark winding road. Tim's words were still echoing in his head, and although he could see his manager looking anxiously sideways at him, he didn't speak. Couldn't.

According to the dubious testimony of a retired Thai prostitute, Admiral Charles Shackleford was a cold-blooded murderer. And tomorrow the papers were going to tell the world about it. Tim had spared none of the gory details scheduled for the morning's editorial and lost no time in telling his highest-earning client that he needed to distance himself from both Victory and her father immediately to avoid any negative impact on his acting career. 'Fans are notoriously fickle,' he'd explained earnestly, ploughing on despite Noah's stony countenance. 'You can't afford this kind of negative publicity at such a crucial stage in your career. Women fall over themselves for you, but it won't take long for your fans to turn against you if they believe you're covering up for a murderer.' Noah hadn't liked the coiled excitement underlying Tim's apparent sincerity. His agent had never liked Noah's relationship with Tory, and though he was trying to hide it, it was pretty obvious that this was news made in heaven as far as Tim was concerned.

To his agent's frustration however, Noah had refused to be drawn and, after instructing the taxi to wait, he left Tim chewing his fingernails and walked quickly up the hill to find

Laurel. Pulling her aside, he briefly explained that an emergency had come up and he needed to contact Tory immediately. She'd know soon enough exactly what the emergency was, but until then, he had no intention of fuelling the inevitable rumours. He asked Laurel if she could wait until he'd left, then inform those who needed to know that he'd be at the next location within the requisite three days. For once the actress didn't ask any questions, simply nodded and gave him a quick kiss on the cheek before pushing him towards his tent.

Ten minutes later, after packing a few things, he was on the road. All he could think about was Tory. Had she tried to get hold of him? Damn, he should have been there for her. What the bloody hell had the Admiral been involved in? Try as he might, he simply couldn't imagine Tory's bluff outspoken father killing anyone in cold blood. As they got ever closer to the coast and civilization, Noah kept glancing down at his phone. As soon as he had a signal, he ordered the taxi to pull over at the next available parking place. As he got out, he waved Tim to stay inside, although he knew his agent would've loved to be party to his conversation with Tory.

The only light came from the moon, and Noah picked his way carefully until he was far enough from the car that there was no risk of anyone overhearing. To his right was a sheer drop, just a small decrepit wall between him and a hundred feet of nothingness. Once he was sure his voice was unlikely to carry to any unwanted ears, he took a deep breath and dialled Tory's number.

∞∞∞

As I stare down at the alien thing ringing in my hand, I feel like I'm going to have a seizure. My heart is thudding in synchronized time to the banging in my head, and the hand holding my mobile is shaking uncontrollably. Squeezing my eyes shut, I swipe to answer and put the phone to my ear.

'Tory?' At the sound of Noah's voice, the crashing in my skull reaches a crescendo, and for a second, I can't speak.

'Tory, is that you?' The anxiety in Noah's voice finally penetrates the symphony in my head, and I murmur his name with a small sob. 'Come on, sweetheart, talk to me,' he continues when I fail to respond with anything remotely legible. 'Are you okay?'

In that second, I realize he already knows. I can hear the sadness, the pity in his voice and it brings me abruptly back to my senses. In a dull voice, I ask him to hold on a second. Then, sitting down on a large boulder, I place the phone carefully down before fishing a scrap of tissue out of my pocket to wipe my eyes and blow my nose. Then I take a couple of shuddering breaths in an effort to calm down before picking up the phone and putting it back to my ear.

'What have you heard?' I try hard to keep my voice from wobbling, roughly scrubbing away the tears sliding down my cheeks.

'Hey, honey,' he answers softly, my efforts to sound in control not fooling him at all, 'Please don't cry. I promise you I'm gonna be on the next flight to England. You don't have to worry anymore, Tory. We'll be together soon, and I'll sort everything.'

'How? How can you sort everything, Noah?' I respond, grief making my voice tight. 'My father's going to be branded a murderer, and there's not a damn thing you or I or anyone else can do about it.'

'Tell me what's happened,' he counters gently, causing the tears to flow harder.

'What have you heard?' I shove the tissue hard into my running nose as I repeat the question.

'Only that some dodgy old hooker has accused your old man of putting an abrupt end to her pimp of a husband.' His voice says he doesn't believe the story for one minute and for a couple of heady seconds, my heart swells at his loyalty, and I allow myself a brief vision of us getting through this together. Then reality comes crashing back in. Sighing, I quickly recount my father's highly abbreviated version of events.

'The problem is, I know there's more to it than that, but Dad just won't speak to me. He seems determined to take the blame for something I don't think he did, but I have no idea why.'

'Tory, listen to me sweetheart, just stay inside the Admiralty until I can get there. Don't speak to anyone, and don't answer the phone to anyone except me. I promise we'll sort this out. I have people I can contact, people who'll help.'

My heart judders sickly at the thought of Noah getting involved in my father's mess, being pulled down into a web of lies going back nearly half a century. His name will be dragged through the mud until his career is nothing but a bitter memory. I know I can't let that happen. Taking a deep breath, I plunge ahead before I lose my nerve.

'Noah you can't come to Dartmouth. The press will be all over the place. They'll hang, draw and quarter you, you know they will. You can't be anywhere near me or my father.'

'I don't give a flying fuck what reporters say about me, and you know that, Tory. I'm coming home to you. We'll get through this together.' His voice is hard and authoritative, attempting to batter down my objections. For a nanosecond, I bask in the knowledge that he believes his home to be where I am, and then I ruthlessly shove it down. How long will he continue to love me when his acting career is in tatters? At what point will he start pointing the finger of blame in my direction? I can't bear the thought of what we've had disintegrating into bitter recriminations and accusations.

'Noah, stop,' I say quietly as he pauses to draw breath. I can almost feel his frustration, his need to make things right. In the end though, I can't face telling him it's over. 'I'm not in Dartmouth,' I say instead. 'Dad and I left yesterday to get ahead of the vultures.'

'Then where are you?' His voice is still commanding, but now I can hear the anguish underneath it. He knows. He can feel me pulling away.

I take a deep breath, then, 'I can't tell you where we are, Noah. You have to stay away, for both our sakes.'

'Bullshit,' he explodes, and my heart contracts sharply at the raw anger in his voice. 'Don't shut me out, Tory. I need to see you, and even if you won't tell me where you are, I swear, I'll find you.'

Against my will, hope surges through me. The prospect of seeing Noah again, even if it's only for a few minutes is simply too much to resist. 'I'm in Scotland,' I say finally, faintly, 'About an hour and a half from Glasgow.' There's a silence, and I can almost see Noah's frowning incredulity on the other end of the line. 'Ok,' he says at length, just as I think he's going to hang up. 'Text me the post code, and I'll let you know when I've landed in Glasgow.'

'If anybody recognizes you...' I begin, only to be cut off with a curt, 'Stop fretting, Tory. No one will recognize me from Adam. You know I've done this before, right?'

'I know,' I whisper, 'I'm so sorry, Noah.' Unbidden, the tears begin flowing again, and I sniffle miserably down the phone. 'I'll be there as quick as I can,' he says softly, 'I love you, Tory, and as the Admiral would say, "This is nothing but a fart in a thunderstorm."' I laugh tearfully as he repeats my father's words in the same blunt English accent. 'I love you too,' I murmur back before realizing he's already disconnected the call.

Burying my head in my hands, I finally allow the tears to come unchecked. Dotty jumps up at me, shivering anxiously, and I simply gather her warm body to me and cry harder into her fur. In fact, my bawling is so loud there's a danger I might wake Mrs. Buchannan's ghostly Lady as well as her entire extended family, but I can't seem to stop.

I so want to believe that seeing Noah again will put everything right. The problem is, deep in my heart, I know that it won't.

I'm not sure, but I think it might be morning. Without opening my eyes, I experimentally move my eyeballs towards the source of light before resolving never to move them again. There's a dull thudding in my head which sounds suspiciously like the theme tune to *Jaws*, and the inside of my mouth feels as though it's been used as a toilet by some small nocturnal rodent, before doubling up as its grave. I try to move my arms and legs and wonder if I did a cross country run before bed last night.

Suddenly, a weird noise comes from above my head, and for a second, I think I've been abducted by aliens. Then it comes again, and I realize it's the sound of Dotty's snoring. Groaning, I turn over to block out the brightness and try to piece together what happened after I finished on the phone to Noah. Then I remember the nearly full bottle of port I consumed as I sat by the dying embers of the Great Hall fire, the star guest at my very own self-pity party for one.

I actually think I might be dying.

The sudden knock at the door reverberates deep inside my brain like some kind of sonic boom. 'Go away.' My voice is cracked and hoarse, causing me to briefly speculate as to whether the rodent in question might actually have been the size of a large guinea pig.

Despite my less-than-sparkling welcome, the door opens, and I unglue my eyelids to see my best friend, looking disgustingly bright eyed and bushy tailed. 'How are you feeling,' she yells, or that's how it seems to my sensitive ears.

'Just put me down and be done with it,' I mumble, figuring that if self-pity has got me this far, why change it now. My uncaring, so-called BFF laughs at my pain. How come I never realized what a cold, cold heart she has?

She plonks herself down on the side of the bed causing it to pitch like the Titanic, and my faithless dog adds to the stomach-churning rolling motion as she clambers callously over me to get to her. 'Here,' Kit says, holding out some revolting green concoction in a large glass, 'A present from Aileen. She says it's the best hangover cure this side of the Erskine Bridge.'

'How does she know I have a hangover?' I ask, easing myself up and taking the glass from her grudgingly.

'Are you joking?' She wiggles her eyebrows at me. 'Don't you remember anything from last night?'

'Not a lot.' I take a small sip of the disgusting mixture and only narrowly avoid projectile vomiting all over Kit's clean white t-shirt. Taking a deep breath, I close my eyes and will my traitorous stomach to stop its roiling. After a minute or so, it does seem a little better, and I open my eyes again, this time to see my best friend regarding me compassionately. Tears, never very far away, prickle at the back of my eyelids. At the moment, cold and callous is what I need if I'm not going to break down again. Taking another hesitant sip, I look down at myself and note I'm still wearing my shirt from yesterday, although my jeans appear to be missing. 'Who put me to bed?' I question with a frown.

'You really don't remember do you?' Kit shakes her head before enlightening me. As she speaks, I change my mind; compassion is good – along with ignorance.

It seems that practically everyone in the Tower heard my wailing and weeping at two in the morning, but unfortunately for me, first on the scene was Jason Buchannan. I wince as Kit describes what happened in full technicolour. I'd like to say my bawling was due to the intense pressure I've been under over the last three days, and I suppose it was, in a way, but apparently, I was bemoaning, loudly, the fact that the bottle of port was empty as Jason arrived on the scene.

'He totally behaved like a complete prick,' Kit says before launching into the lurid details. Apparently, my best friend arrived on the scene just as Jason was prizing the empty port bottle out of my hand, and for a couple of seconds she was actually concerned that he intended to hit me over the head with it.

'Do you know how old this bottle of port is?' he spat to Kit through gritted teeth when she asked him what the hell he thought he was doing. 'It's *one hundred and fifty years* old.'

'Well, it's about time somebody drank it then,' was Kit's unsympathetic response. 'Can't you see that my friend is going through a terrible time?'

 She was interrupted by my hiccupping echo, 'izz really, really tebb... terbl... telab... bad.'

It appears that those memorable words were the sum total of my contribution to the conversation, as once I'd mumbled them, I keeled over and passed out. After hurriedly checking to see I was still breathing, Kit continued her tirade. 'I don't think you have a compassionate bone in your body, Mr. Buchannan, and what's more you've made it clear from the moment you arrived that you do not want us here. But I can assure you, we are here for a reason, one I'm sure you will understand later on today, but until then, just look at my friend. Can't you see how much pain she's in...?' Evidently, at this point, she was interrupted in mid flow by my snoring.

'Not nearly as much as she's likely to be in when she wakes

up,' was Jason's thick-skinned response. 'Are you going to help me get her to bed or just stand there nagging?' Luckily, before Kit could respond to *that* insensitive retort, my father appeared with Pickles in tow, having been woken up by Freddy, who'd sensibly opted for waking up the Admiral rather than joining in the mudslinging going on below.

Dotty, who until that point had been curled up next to me (she obviously didn't care whether I was sober or not), jumped up with a loud bark to greet Pickles. At the noise, I apparently leapt up and promptly fell over her, straight into Jason's arms.

'What the bloody hell are you up to Victory?' My father hurried downstairs and none-too gently yanked me out of Jason's arms. 'I'll take it from here,' he puffed, trying vainly to support me while endeavouring to wind my arm around his shoulders. 'Bollocking hell, have you put weight on girl?' he gasped as I leaned against him, a dead weight. It didn't help that both Pickles and Dotty were dancing around him thinking this was a new kind of game. 'Get out of the bloody way,' he roared in the end.

Just as Kit tried to take my other arm, Jason sighed irritably and shoved his body in the way. 'Let me take her other arm,' he said crossly, 'There's no way you're going to get her up the stairs on your own.'

By this point, I am cringing internally and wave Kit to please stop, I've heard enough.
'Just tell me I didn't give away why we're here,' I groan, head in my hands.

'No, you didn't, Tory, but it doesn't really matter anymore because you're now headline news as predicted.' I look up quickly, only to shut my eyes as a wave of nausea hits me along with a shooting pain like someone is sticking a skewer in each eyeball. 'Oh God, I'm such a prat. Why on earth did I get hammered with this hanging over my head?'

'This hanging over your head is precisely why you did get hammered,' Kit retorts, standing up and placing a reluctant Dotty onto the floor.

'I really don't think I'll be able to look Jason Buchannan in the eyes again,' I moan to her back as she straightens up again.

'Yeah, well that shouldn't be a problem, we're waiting for the eviction notice as we speak.'
Unbelievably, I sense slight disappointment in her tone, and I want to explore it further, but just as I open my mouth, I glance down at my watch.

'OMG, it's nearly lunchtime. Why didn't you tell me? Noah might have tried to call.' I stagger out of bed and grab my things. 'Where's Dad, have you seen him?'

'Not yet, I'll go and tell him his daughter's finally awake and relatively sober.'

My head has moved on from *Jaws* to the theme tune from *Ghostbusters* as I hop around the bedroom trying to pull on my jeans.

'I take it you managed to speak with Noah last night then?' Kit's voice is casual which doesn't fool me at all. I sink to a chair, giving up on trying to put my clothes on standing. 'Yeah, we talked, for all the good it did. He's determined to see me. Wants us to ride it out together.' I laugh mirthlessly. 'He might have changed his mind after he's seen the headlines this morning though.'

'You should listen to him, Tory,' Kit says earnestly, placing her hand on my shoulder to help me pull on my blouse. 'He's a good guy. He won't leave you just because the shit's hit the fan.'

'I know he won't, Kitty Kat, that's the problem. I've got to do it for him. You know what this will do to his career. I won't be responsible for ruining his life.'

'Don't you think that's his decision to make?' Kit returns softly, although I can't help but note that she doesn't argue about the ruination of his life bit.

Sighing, I stand up, more or less dressed. 'We won't survive it Kit. You know what the press are like. Once they get hold of a story, they're like a pack of wolves; they'll keep sniffing and sniffing until they manage to dig up every bit of dirt.'

'But you said your father's innocent. Surely that counts for something.'

'Not as far as all the bloodthirsty newshounds are concerned. They don't care whether someone's innocent or guilty. They just want a juicy story – and let's be honest, they don't get much juicier than this.' I pick up the glass containing Aileen's hideous concoction, and shuddering, I down it in one go.

'Time to face the music.'

In the end, the only two people around when we get down to the Great Hall are Freddy and Mabel. So engrossed in the events unfolding on the TV screen, they fail to notice us at first until Dotty runs up to Freddy and jumps into his lap, for once completely ignored by a very subdued Pickles seated on the floor between them. As I approach, they both look up, and I can't help but notice how pale they both are.

'Where's Dad?' I ask again quietly, sitting on the sofa opposite. There'll be plenty of time to watch the horror show later.

'Oh, Victory,' Mabel raises red-rimmed eyes. 'They left in the early hours. He's written you a note.' She pushes an envelope towards me before sniffing back into a tissue. Looking down, I recognize my father's handwriting, and my heart clenches painfully as I tear it open.

I'm just about to start reading when Aileen bustles in with a welcome pot of coffee. As she puts the tray down, she nods towards the TV screen with the cryptic comment, 'Tatties o'wer the side and no mistake hen.' Then, with a quick squeeze of my shoulder, she heads back towards the kitchen. Reluctantly, I turn back to the note in my hand.

Dear Victory

Hugo and I have gone to see what's to be done. You can stay at Bloodstone Tower for as long as you like, pay no attention to young Buchannan – he might be all teeth, tits and toenails, but he won't give you any trouble. Make sure Mabel gets home safely, she's looking after Pickles while I'm gone – thought you'd probably have enough on your plate.

I'll be in touch as soon as I can. Until then, keep your head down, girl. It's all a load of bollocks, and I promise I'll get it sorted somehow.

And don't give up on the Yank. He's a good bloke, Victory, and he'll come through for you if you let him.

Your loving father
xxx

Chapter Nine

Forty Years Ago...

HMS Hermes rested quietly at anchor. It was three o'clock in the morning, and all was silent apart from the occasional murmur of conversation between the officer of the watch and the lookout. Lieutenants Charles Shackleford and Hugo Buchannan were sound asleep in their cabin. Both considered themselves extremely lucky that their adventure into the seedier side of Thai life the evening before hadn't found its way up to their Captain, and they intended it to stay that way.

Their guide, Kulap, had been paid off handsomely on return to the ship, and Doris had been sent off with a flea in his ear. 'I don't care who the bloody hell you are, but you breathe a word of tonight's bollocking fiasco, and I'll string you up the yard arm myself.' Charles Shackleford hadn't minced his words to the sub lieutenant who'd given a subdued nod, his earlier cockiness replaced by white-faced anxiety. Jimmy hadn't needed telling at all – he'd simply saluted smartly then scarpered.

Suddenly, the door to the cabin creaked open slightly. 'Psst, Sir, are you awake? I need to speak with you urgently.' There was a brief silence while the speaker waited to see if his urgent whisper had jolted either lieutenant awake, but as the sound of snoring continued unabated, the door was pushed open further, and the strained face of Doris peered around it into the darkened cabin. After waiting another couple of seconds, the sub lieutenant slipped into the room and crept towards the shadowed bunks where he hovered uncertainly between the two, trying to decide which of the lumpy outlines was which officer. Not that it mattered he supposed - he was going to get hauled over the coals whoever he woke. In the end, he tiptoed to the bunk on the right and bent over the still form until his face was in the lieutenant's ear. 'Sir,' he whispered as loudly as he dared.

Charles Shackleford opened his eyes to see a phantom no more than six inches away from his face. Yelling, 'Bloody hell, it's a ghost,' his fist shot out catching the would-be ghoul directly on his surprisingly solid nose. The force of the punch sent the apparition stumbling backwards into the other bunk where it landed with a loud thud.

At the impact, Hugo Buchannan shot up in bed shouting, 'We're under attack Char...' before almost braining himself on the shelf above him which wobbled ominously before cashing in its chips and crashing, books and all onto the lieutenant's head.

Both officers stared wildly at Doris, now sitting on the floor holding his nose. 'I dink it bite be bwoken,' he mumbled trying to stem the steady flow of blood using the tail of his shirt.

'Well, if it isn't, it bloody soon will be.' Charles was the first to recover his wits and climbed out of bed, resisting the urge to give the young sub lieutenant a black eye to match. Turning on the light, he grabbed a towel, and shoved it unceremoniously towards Doris before helping to free Hugo's bunk from the littered debris. 'What the bollocking hell were you thinking, man?' he asked, sweeping the fallen books onto the floor, 'Have you got cotton wool for brains between your bloody ears?'

'I deeded to dalk do you,' Doris muttered behind the towel. 'I dink I bite be in big dwubble.' Charles frowned and looked over towards Hugo who was still sitting nursing his head.

81

'Och, ye numpty, ah pure wallaped ma heid aff that bloody shelf,' was his only response, the trauma obviously bringing out the Scottish in him.

'What sort of trouble?' Charles turned back to Doris who still had his head buried in the towel. Frowning, he sighed unsympathetically. 'Here you donkey, let me have a look.' Yanking the cloth away, he none too gently felt around Doris's nose, ignoring the subsequent squeak of pain, and pronounced, 'Not broken, just bruised.' Then he thrust a cluster of tissues at Doris before continuing, 'Shove some of this up your hooter, then tell us what this is all about so we can all get some bloody shut eye.'

There was a short silence punctuated by Hugo moaning about possible concussion while Doris wadded as much tissue as possible up each nostril. By the time he finally looked up, both officers were much more alert, seated on the edge of their respective bunks, waiting impatiently for him to elaborate.

Doris swallowed nervously as he wiped his bloody hands on the rest of the tissue, stalling for time. 'They stole my wallet,' he muttered sullenly eventually. 'And you woke us up for *that*?' is Charles's unsympathetic response, 'You've got as much chance of getting the bloody thing back as I have of becoming king of England.'

Doris could see that irritation was fast overcoming any slight compassion the two officers might have had, so he took a deep breath, knowing he had to cut to the chase pretty sharpish. 'I left my passport at that place,' he rushed at length. Charles and Hugo stared at him silently, their identical disbelieving expressions speaking volumes. Without giving the officers time to give voice to their incredulity, which Doris had no doubt would be loud and even more painful, the young sub lieutenant stammered on, 'I took it in case I got into trouble, sort of a failsafe if you know what I mean…' He stumbled to a halt in the face of their continued stillness, then, taking a deep breath, he delivered the punch line. 'The thing is, it's got my real name on it.'

Chapter Ten

As I sit staring at the note, my mind is a complete blank. I have absolutely no idea what to do next. I know what I want to do, and that's to crawl back into my bed with the curtains tightly closed and shut out the world. I look over at the TV screen, now busy showing "the rest of today's news" and notice that along the bottom of the screen in a continuous loop are the words…

Breaking News… Victory Shackleford, unlikely girlfriend of Hollywood heartthrob Noah Westbrook is today facing the possibility that her father Charles Shackleford will, in all likelihood, be charged with first degree murder. The shocking allegations could well see the end of her fairy-tale relationship with the actor, which developed while he was filming on location in her father's house. Neither Mr. Westbrook nor Ms. Shackleford have so far been available to comment… Stay tuned for the full story…

With a horrible sense of déjà vu, I climb wearily off the sofa and turn off the TV. 'I'm going outside to see if Noah's tried to call me, I won't be long.'

As I pass, Mabel catches hold of my hand, holding me still briefly. 'Your father didn't do this horrible thing they're accusing him of my dear, just remember that, and have faith.'

I smile tremulously down at her kind, earnest face, wondering how I could ever have thought she wasn't suitable stepmother material, then, I squeeze her hand in thanks and gently pull myself free. 'Come on, Dotspot, Pickles, let's go for a walk.'

Ten minutes later, I'm throwing stones for the two dogs while waiting for my phone to ring. Noah left an answer phone message in the early hours to let me know he'd be landing in Glasgow around twelve forty-five pm. The time's now twelve thirty and I still can't decide what to say to him when he calls. Suggesting he comes here would be the easiest thing to do, although we won't exactly be alone – but then maybe that's a good thing. My mind keeps replaying everything over and over again in a continuous loop of thoughts much like the words along the bottom of the TV screen. When the phone finally rings, I'm no further forward, and answer the phone simply to hear his voice.

'Where are you, Tory?' His voice is tender but brusque, giving me no time to back out of seeing him by wasting time in small talk. In the end, it's easier to stop fighting and just give him the address and post code. 'Why am I not surprised that your old man hightails it up to somewhere with a name like Bloodstone Tower,' is his only dry response. I have no idea how he intends to get here, or how he's going to find it – it's not exactly on any tourist route.

It's enough that he's coming.

As I make my way back to the house, I hear raised voices coming from inside the Great Hall, and my heart sinks. Jason Buchannan. I'd forgotten about our boorish host. Maybe if I hover out here for long enough, he'll get over the fact that he's harbouring the daughter of a potential fugitive and bugger off.

Picking Dotty up, I peep around the half open door to see Kit, Freddy and Jason clustered around the dining table. Mabel is nowhere to be seen. Standing quietly with my ear to the small opening, I unashamedly eavesdrop on the conversation.

'I don't care if they've been friends since nappies, I don't want my father mixed up in whatever bloody mischief Charles Shackleford has got himself involved in.'

'Have you ever thought your father could be involved in all this so-called bloody mischief too?' Strangely, it's Freddy's voice that answers, sounding tight lipped and angry. 'There's no way the Admiral would drag Tory all the way up here without good reason.'

'Way to go, Freddy, good point, well made.' I nod my head sagely even though the only witness to it is Dotty (and ignoring the fact that my father is quite capable of dragging me halfway around the world on nothing more than a slight whim). 'Come on, answer that, you toad,' I mutter, waiting to see if Jason is able to shed any further light on the mystery.

There's a short silence, then Jason's next words take the wind out of my sails completely. 'You're probably right,' is all he says with a frustrated sigh. 'The last time I was clearing out my father's old mail, I came across a note referring to "The Hermes Incident". It didn't say much, but both the Admiral and my father were mentioned, and someone called Noon?'

I gasp as Jimmy's name is mentioned – so he *was* involved - and decide it's time to take part in the conversation. Putting Dotty down, I push open the door fully and allow the dogs to rush in as though I've just got back. 'What's that about the Hermes incident?' I ask innocently, as I walk towards them.

Jason looks over at me irritably. 'How long have you been standing there?' he responds rudely, causing me to wonder if his dislike is confined to anyone with the name of Shackleford. I shrug, determined not to give anything away, particularly about Jimmy, whilst at the same time pumping him for as much information as possible. I glance towards Kit who gets it immediately and interrupts Freddy when it looks as though he's going to connect the dots.

'Well, it looks like you know more than we do.' She shrugs. 'But at least your father is not actually being implicated in murder. For now,' she adds darkly. Jason's frown indicates that this possibility has actually occurred to him, and I decide to turn the screw a little more.

'I imagine they're going to want to take your dad in for questioning at least, especially if he was around when whatever happened, happened.' Jason opens his mouth, obviously intending to argue, then unexpectedly closes it again. Closing his eyes, he runs his hand through his hair angrily.

'Dad hardly ever talks about his time in the Royal Navy. The only person he's ever kept in touch with since my mum died is your father. But I've got to say they don't appear to like each other very much.'

'Like father, like son,' I resist the urge to mutter, saying brusquely instead, 'Well if it's not undying friendship that keeps them in contact, it stands to reason it must be something else – and I get the feeling we're going to be enlightened pretty soon as to exactly what.'

Eventually, Jason makes the decision to follow our two fathers down to London in case he's needed. I want to ask what he thinks he might be needed for, and, if it's another blistering lecture, whether that's likely to add anything positive to their situation. In the end though, I decide that a meeting between Mr. Poker Face and Noah is probably best avoided at this particular point in time, and while my father might not thank me for it, Jason Buchannan is best away from Bloodstone Tower during the brief time Noah is here.

And I'm determined that it will be brief, however much I might want it to be otherwise.

As he leaves, Jason actually stops in front of me to say stiffly, 'I'm sorry we seem to have started off on the wrong foot, Ms. Shackleford, but my father would like you to know that you and your friends are welcome to stay here for as long as you like.' He pauses and glances over towards Kit with a peculiar regret in his eyes, before continuing quietly, 'I hope everything works out for you, Victory; however, I'd be very grateful if you'd try not to kill my grandmother while I'm gone...'

The afternoon seems to go on forever. No further information has been released since the headlines of this morning, so the various TV channels have taken to rehashing all the lurid details of our last brush with notoriety, complete with lots of gorgeous studio shots of Noah and Gaynor Andrews and equally hideous, (though thankfully grainy) pictures of me, which worryingly seem to have been mostly taken whilst I was in my tatty old dressing gown. Maybe the swanky new gates at the Admiralty are not quite as foolproof as we thought...

Kit, Freddy and Mabel keep wanting to talk about my relationship with Noah, with my two friends firmly of the opinion that I should hang on to him until I'm prized off with a claw hammer and Mabel helpfully adding that I should stick to him like shit to a shovel... Aileen keeps coming in with a never-ending stream of coffee and shortbread - mainly I think so she can keep abreast of the most exciting affair to hit Bloodstone Tower since the Lady's kinsmen were thrown out of the window. I'm tempted to tell her to just sit down and join in the discussion, but since I can't really understand anything she says, I decide it will only complicate the situation. Of old Mrs. Buchannan there is no sign – I don't know whether to be relieved or concerned...

After two hours of my friends' well-meaning advice, I'm ready to throw myself into the loch. I remind them all, sparing an apologetic look towards Mabel, that my father is alleged to have murdered a *prostitute* (not that that's better or worse than murdering anyone else – but it has to be said, it provides a much juicier story given the fact that he'd been in a brothel to actually commit the heinous crime…) My nerves are now wound up tighter than a monkey's nuts, as my father would say. I keep trying to work out what time Noah is likely to get here, and every time Dotty cocks her head on one side to listen, my heart judders and I just want to be sick.

In the end, I jump up with the mumbled excuse that Noah may be trying to call me, which is perfectly true. As I'm leaving the room with the two dogs in tow (Pickles appears determined not to let me out of his sight), Freddy calls my name. I look back at his uncharacteristically serious face. 'If he hurts you, Tory, he'll have me to answer to.' I picture the two of them, Noah and Freddy, squaring up to each other and almost feel like smiling, although I'm sure, from his earnest expression, that that wasn't Freddy's intention.

'He won't hurt me, Freddy,' I say softly. 'It's much more likely to be the other way round…'

It's another hour and a half before I actually receive a text from Noah to tell me his cab's about twenty minutes away. I resist the urge to ask if the taxi's taken him the scenic route – maybe via The Shetland Isles – seeing as it's taken so long, but I don't think this is the right time for sarcasm. So, I fiddle with my phone a bit, and in the end just text back some kisses.

My nerves are now going into overdrive. I look down at myself for the first time since my undignified start to the day and suddenly realize I'm not exactly looking my best. Baggy shirt, jeans and trainers – not exactly sex on legs. Things must be bad if Freddy's passed over the opportunity to make a bitchy comment about my chosen attire. Still, looking good is not the objective here – making Noah see sense is, and when he sees me for the first time in weeks looking like this, he might just wonder what on earth all the fuss was about. I just wish I could stop the ache in my heart at the thought of him not loving me anymore.

I'm listening for the noise of a car, so in the end I completely miss Noah's arrival on foot. Dotty's the first to spot him standing in the shadows of an overgrown azalea bush and abandons her sniffing to dash up to him barking joyfully, closely followed by Pickles, trailing behind her at a more sedate pace.

Rooted to the spot, heart threatening to burst out of my chest, I gaze at him helplessly, as always, completely blindsided anew by his sheer masculine beauty. He bends down to fuss the two dogs gamboling around him enthusiastically, then straightens up to regard me steadily, silently. After a couple of seconds, he begins moving slowly, almost predatorily, in my direction, and before I can stop myself, I take an involuntary step backwards, intimidated by the intensity of his gaze. But despite my nervousness, every part of me is springing to vibrant life as he walks determinedly towards me, and when he finally halts, a couple of feet away, it's me who takes the final two steps with an incoherent whisper, the longing and need to be in his arms pushing everything else aside.

Without taking his eyes off my face, Noah drops his bag, and raises his hand to gently stroke my wet cheek. Up until now, I have no idea I've been crying. With a groan, he yanks me against his chest, his mouth opening hungrily against mine. As if in a dream, I feel his hands sliding over my back and hips, pulling me to him as if he's trying to absorb my body into his. Incredibly, a shudder runs through his tall frame as with a small whimper I completely surrender and arch into him, wrapping my arms around his neck.

Lost in a world of hunger and need, I almost stagger when Noah abruptly tears his mouth away from mine and stares down at me in silence. His shoulders are heaving as though he's been running, and his incredible blue eyes are heavy and slumberous with desire. For me.

I lean forward and press myself against him, not yet ready to face what I know is coming, but he holds me back and gently disengages my arms from around his neck. 'We need to talk,' he murmurs raggedly at my whispered protest. His face is determined, despite the hoarseness of his voice and, eventually, with a small sigh, I rest my head against his chest briefly before pulling away.

Gathering my wits together, I take refuge in small talk as he picks up his bag. 'Where's the taxi?' I ask for something to say.

'I got out of the cab a mile or so down the road. I didn't want him to see my destination just in case he recognised me.'

'Do you think he did?' My voice is high-pitched with sudden alarm until Noah shakes his head.

'I be an actor, Tory,' he responds with a very credible Irish accent, 'Sure people see what tey be wantin' ta see.' He completes the transformation with a cap and sunglasses, previously lying discarded in the top of the bag, and I can't help but laugh, easing the tension.

'Come on then, Paddy, let me show you Bloodstone Tower.'

In the end, it's another twenty minutes before we go inside. Noah is completely fascinated by the tower and insists on exploring right around the outside before venturing into the Great Hall. The dogs are happy to oblige, and of course, I'm more than happy to put off our "talk" and simply enjoy the bittersweet feeling of watching Noah's characteristic, almost boyish, enthusiasm for anything new and interesting.

By the time we get to the inside, it's nearly six o'clock and the Great Hall is empty, late afternoon sunlight streaming in a myriad of colours through the mullioned windows. 'Wow,' is his only comment as he stares around. I smile, watching his beautiful, animated face, determined to commit this moment to memory, whatever happens after.

'Bloody uncanny. It's just like Braveheart. All you need is a skirt, and you'd be Mel Gibson.' Freddy's droll comment is made from the depths of one of the sofas fronting the huge fireplace. I was wrong, the room isn't empty – I can only blame Dotty's failure to spot the fact on her complete infatuation with Noah. Just like her owner.

Laughing good naturedly, Noah strides towards Freddy with no hesitation. 'Hey, buddy, how's it going? Good to see you again, just wish it was in happier circumstances. Thanks a bunch for taking care of Tory.' They shake hands just as Aileen comes in to join the party. On seeing Noah, she stops, flustered, and hurriedly wipes her hands on her floury apron, all the while staring with her mouth open and closing like a fish.

'Noah, this is Aileen. She's been doing a fabulous job of looking after us over the last couple of days.' I watch fascinated as Noah does that thing he does – the slow, unbelievably sexy smile that starts around his eyes. By the time he's finished, Aileen has gone a delightful shade of pink and is standing stock still, gazing at the actor while muttering, 'Keep the heid Aileen, keep the heid.' Noah looks at me, and I shrug – he's the expert on accents, not me…

Luckily, at that moment, Dotty makes up for her earlier slip by barking, seconds before the door to the upstairs is pushed open by Kit. 'Noah!' she says simply, and I wonder if I'm the only one who can hear the relief in her voice. She hurries across the room and gives him a hug, this time leaving no doubt to everyone present of her delight at seeing him. I'm beginning to realize that I'm really not going to get any support at all in my attempts to distance myself from Noah.

Feeling suddenly heartsick, I start walking towards the staircase. 'If you'll come with me, I'll show you our room.' I'm aware that my voice is a bit sharp, almost petulant, but I stifle the urge to look back. I really don't want to see them all rolling their eyes at my juvenile behaviour.

I hear Noah's footsteps behind me as I open the door to the dark stone stairs winding to the upper levels, but I don't look at him, just leave him to follow. Dotty manages to slip through the door just before it closes behind him and dashes upwards to lead the way. Once in our room, the little dog launches herself on to the bed, and looks back at Noah, tail wagging happily. God, I so want to do the same... Instead, I walk over to the window and rest my head on the cool glass. 'Well, I'm obviously staying the night. That's something at least,' Noah says drily, 'And there's no sofa.'

The last is said softly, intimately, and the insinuation in his words sends shockwaves of dizzying emotions racing through me. Taking a deep breath, I force the traitorous sensations down and turn round to face him. 'You were right, we do have to talk.' My voice is shaking. I know what I have to do, but it's so hard to say the words – I don't think self-sacrifice agrees with me. Noah simply stands and watches me, arms folded, expression blank. 'Noah, I..'

'Stop.' His interruption is sudden and harsh, causing me to flinch slightly. Although almost imperceptible, he sees my reaction and softens his tone. 'I know I said we need to talk, but let's have this one night together Tory. Tomorrow, we can discuss the fallout from the allegations against your father. Just one night – can we do that?'

'No,' I want to scream at him, 'We can't. One night's not enough, it will never be enough.' Instead, I blink back threatened tears, and, swallowing back the lump in my throat, I finally nod my head, not trusting myself to speak.

Sensing my turmoil, he walks over to me silently, and gently folds me into his arms. I stiffen for a second, then relax against his hard warmth. The smell of soap and cloves that is pure Noah enfolds me, promising a safe haven filled with love and laughter, and even though I know it's a fantasy, I finally let myself go.

By the time I finish crying, Noah's shirt front is completely soaked. At some point, he guides me towards the bed, lying down on it and gathering my unresisting body tightly against his chest. As my storm of sobbing finally begins to abate, I become aware of his hand gently stroking my hair. Hiccupping slightly, I lift my head from his chest and look up. 'I'm so sorry,' I whisper, sniffing, 'You know I'm not normally this pathetic, it's just...' My voice dries up as he brushes his lips against my temple.

'You don't have to apologize to me, Tory,' he murmurs huskily. 'I love you, and I'll never willingly leave you.' Heart thudding, I open my mouth to respond, but he gently places his finger over my lips. 'Tomorrow,' he says firmly. 'Now try to get some sleep before dinner, you've got a long night ahead of you.' I laugh softly at his mock lascivious tone. As I drift off to sleep, the last thing I feel is Dotty, determinedly squeezing herself between the two of us and resting her head on Noah's chest, sighing contentedly.

They always say that dogs take after their owners...

Chapter Eleven

We all gather in the Great Hall at seven thirty, and against all odds, dinner is great fun. As the wine flows, Noah is on top form, telling everyone about the monsters in his new movie. 'So, are they like sort of furry aliens?' asks Freddy, 'You know, like the twenty foot dentally challenged uglies in the Sigourney Weaver movie - but with hair?'

'You mean like the abdominal snowman?' pipes up Mabel helpfully, looking around us in bewilderment when we all fall about laughing.

'James Cameron's not the director, is he?' Freddy continues excitedly when the giggles have subsided. Noah shakes his head with a smile,

'No, and neither is Ridley Scott before you ask. The director of *Nocturne* is a new guy on the block. This movie could pretty much make or break him.' Listening to Noah's animated voice discussing his new movie simply highlights just how much he loves what he does, and watching the others respond to his undeniable charisma slowly strengthens my resolve. I will not be responsible for taking all of that away from him. All I need to do is to convince him I'm right. Tomorrow...

After dinner, Noah and I leave the others playing cards to take the dogs for a walk. Freddy's enthusiastic suggestion that we could all do with some fresh air is ruthlessly stamped on by

Kit's foot – literally, and I smile at her gratefully before following Noah out of the door. The last thing I hear before the door shuts behind us is, 'Bloody hell, Freddy, you really are a complete plonker sometimes,' and I laugh softly, causing Noah to turn back with raised eyebrows.

'It's nothing,' I murmur, waving him on. 'Just Kit and Freddy having a slight disagreement.'

The evening is balmy and warm, only the gentle splash of waves breaking against the shore interrupting the stillness. The midges have turned in for the night and the sky is completely clear and full of stars. I take Noah's hand to guide him and silently we wander down to the edge of the loch. As we reach the shore, the landscape opens to reveal the shadowy outlines of the mountains rising up on the other side, and I hear Noah's indrawn breath. 'Beautiful, isn't it?' I whisper, reluctant to break the quiet.

I can just about make out his answering nod as he lets go of my hand to move closer and wrap his arm around my shoulders. We walk in companionable silence along the loch side as Dotty and Pickles sniff at the ground and take it in turns to chase invisible rabbits. After a few minutes we arrive at the small landing on the side of the loch, and in unspoken agreement, sit down side by side on the rickety bench. Resting my head on Noah's shoulder, I wonder if I'll ever again experience this sense of belonging I have when I'm with him.

After a few seconds, I feel his head turn towards me and gently kiss the top of my head. When I look up, the midnight intensity of his eyes holds me spellbound, until he finally bends his head, lips finding mine in a featherlight touch. The shock of the contact is electrifying, and the kiss quickly turns into something deeper as I open my mouth under his. 'I need to take you to bed,' he whispers huskily after long minutes, unless you want me to take you right here.' A knot of pure sensation slams into the pit of my stomach at the thought of making love to Noah under the stars. Luckily, Dotty chooses that moment to jump up between us, and I laugh shakily before saying, 'Probably better to choose the bed...'

It's five am, and I'm lying awake listening to Noah's level breathing next to me. Looking over at his peaceful sleeping face, I trace its contours with my eyes, committing every feature to memory.

When we returned to the bedroom last night, Noah undressed me, slowly taking one item of clothing off at a time. At first I was self-conscious, but his fingers brooked no interference as they searched, stroked, caressed, and everywhere they touched, his lips and tongue followed, until I was almost mindless with need. Then trembling, I returned the favour, tracing the hard planes of his chest and finally touching the smooth rigid heat of him until, groaning, he'd pushed me back onto the bed, where at long last we were skin to skin, his body hot and heavy, a seductive weight that tormented and teased, until he finally relented and took us both to oblivion.

Leaning up on one elbow, I watch him sleep and feel my love for him well up until it almost overwhelms me. How on earth am I going to be able to let him go? With a small sigh, almost a sob, I turn away from him, intending to get out of bed to fetch Dotty who's spent the night with Kit.

Suddenly, a hand clamps on my arm, halting my movement and pulling me backwards. With a small scream, I find myself suddenly wedged under a solid muscled chest. 'Where do you think you're going, Victory Shackleford,' he murmurs silkily in between placing small featherlight kisses onto my neck. Gasping, I instinctively arch myself up to get closer as he trails the kisses to the side of my mouth.

'Nowhere,' I just have time to whisper, before his mouth closes hungrily over mine, and we push the world away for a little while longer.

'You know we can't keep avoiding the subject,' I force myself to say to him later after we're both able to think clearly again. My head is resting on his chest, my hand idly tracing a figure of eight through the smattering of dark hair. The abrupt comment stills his hand, up to now busy stroking softly, comfortingly up and down my back. Then he sighs.

'Okay,' he says flatly, 'You start.'

I so do not want this conversation, but then I recall his animation during the banter at dinner last night. Taking a deep breath, I try to find the right words. 'Noah, I...' then my throat dries up, and my mind goes into a complete fug.

'Yep, that's my name,' he responds drily when I fail to continue. Lifting my head, I shoot him an irritated look.

'You're really not making this easy for me,' I grouch.

'So, what would you have me do?' he retorts back, 'Just pack up and walk away? That's not who I am, Tory. You know that. I love you, and believe it or not, that means something. We – or rather *I* – allowed the press to get between us last time, and I don't intend to make the same mistake again.' His voice is calm and controlled, but there's an underlying steel beneath, warning me not to push this. But I have to. I'd rather walk away now than watch him fall slowly out of love with me over the coming weeks and months.

'It's not about me and you,' I say, looking up at him earnestly, 'Well, not *just* anyway. You have an amazing career, with millions of adoring fans, but we all know how fickle the public can be. You could lose those fans in an instant if they think you're involved in something dirty and grubby – like murder for example.'

'God, you sound like my agent,' Noah interjects impatiently as I pause for breath.

'But, don't you see, he's right, love,' I respond grimly. 'I could never forgive myself if you lost everything because of me.' I sit up, not daring to look at him as the next words come out in a rush, 'The sooner you distance yourself from my family Noah, the better you'll be.' There, I've finally said it. I squeeze my eyes shut, waiting tensely for the explosion.

Instead, the silence goes on for so long I want to scream, and when he finally does speak, his voice is quiet.

'Yes, I love what I do,' he says softly, achingly, 'but the truth is I love you more. And I'm not prepared to give up what we have based on gossip and scaremongering.'

'You call murder gossip and scaremongering?' I respond tartly, even as my heart swells at his words. Noah waves his hand irritably at my comment.

'We don't know yet whether your father killed anybody. You told me yourself that he denied it when you tackled him. Have you ever known him to lie...?' I interrupt him with an incredulous snort, and he continues quickly before I can butt in, 'I mean about anything like this? Your father's no murderer Tory, but you've got him locked up before he's even been arrested.'

I open my mouth to speak, then stop and rest my head onto my raised knees. Am I being too hasty? I just don't know. I can't seem to think. My mind is picturing Noah's cold remoteness when I confronted him in London. 'I just couldn't bear it if you started hating me again,' I whisper finally. I can feel him sit up behind me a second before he leans forward to put his arms around my shoulders, pulling me back against the warmth of his naked chest.

'I'll never hate you, Tory, and I don't abandon someone I love simply because the going gets tough. I'm not my father.' I frown, momentarily distracted. This is the first time he's ever voluntarily mentioned his father. Whenever I've brought the subject up, he's always deflected it. Intrigued, I turn towards him. 'You've never spoken about your dad before. Why did he leave?'

For a second, I don't think Noah's going to answer, but in the end, all he says is, 'The usual – no money, another baby on the way, greener grass beckoning somewhere else. He just went to work one day and never came home. Mom was worried sick the night he disappeared, spent the whole night on the phone. The police wouldn't do anything until he'd been missing for over twenty-four hours. The company he worked for told mom he'd quit, but they didn't have any idea where he'd gone. They said it was strange that another one of their delivery drivers – a woman – had walked out at the same time. So there we go, you do the math.'

'What did your mum do?'

'The same as every woman who's been abandoned by a douche bag. Got three jobs and did her best to keep a roof over our heads. Luckily, we had great neighbours who looked out for us. I used to spend every day there and when Kim was born, they babysat her too.'

I sit for a second deep in thought and can't help but reflect just how different Noah's childhood was to mine. Even though my father's always been a bit eccentric, I grew up with two parents who both loved me, in an area that was quite simply a paradise for kids. Sighing, I snuggle back against him. 'You've come such a long way Noah. Your mum must have been so proud of you.'

'She was proud of both of us. I know it sounds clichéd, but the biggest reward to being supposedly rich and famous was being able to give her everything she'd missed out on when we were kids.'

'Are you sure your father actually left you? What if something bad happened to him?'

'Oh, he left us alright, and he didn't end up as a John Doe in some morgue.'

'How do you know? Did he contact you?' I know I'm pushing it, but it's so hard to get Noah to open up about his past, and I'm determined to strike while the iron's hot.

'Yep, he crawled out of the woodwork a few years ago. Did an interview on ABC saying how sad he was that we didn't have a relationship. How much he'd missed me, blah, blah, blah.' Noah's voice is becoming flippant, and I can tell he wants to change the subject, so I capitulate and turn my head to kiss him lightly on the lips. His sudden indrawn breath indicates how much just the simple kiss affects him, and I marvel that I'm actually able to do that to him.

Then, as his hands slowly work their way down from my shoulders, I stop thinking altogether.

It's almost lunchtime by the time we finally venture downstairs, and I smile apologetically at Kit as Dotty dances up to me, tail wagging as though I've been away for years. We still haven't come to any decision about the future – or rather I haven't. Noah seems determined to commit professional suicide, no matter what arguments I put in front of him.

'Any news?' I ask my two best friends as we help ourselves to coffee. The mild tone of my question fools neither of them, and my stomach lurches at the glance they exchange. Resisting the urge to scream at them, I force myself to wait, staring expectantly.

'The Admiral offered to turn himself in to the Metropolitan Police this morning, although he hasn't shown up so far. Apparently, the Thai authorities are demanding he be extradited to stand trial for murder.'

'But it happened over forty years ago,' I burst out. 'Surely, they can't just demand extradition now. How on earth will they ever get to the truth? Oh God, I've heard about Thai prisons, how can we even be sure Dad will get a fair trial?' My voice is getting louder as my panic intensifies along with the sick feeling in my stomach. Noah puts his hand over mine, slowly unclenching my fingers with his.

'The UK Government won't simply hand him over, Tory. They'll do their own investigation into the allegations first. Let me see if I can find anything out. I have a few favours I can call in.'

'NO.' I turn to him wildly, gripping his hand. 'You can't get involved, Noah. Please stay out of it. Promise me.' He stares back at me without speaking, a mixture of sympathy and frustration palpable in his silence. I take a deep breath. 'Please, Noah,' I continue more calmly. 'If you love me, then do this for me, or we finish it right now.'

The anger flares in his eyes at my ultimatum, and I just want to curl into a ball and cry. But I know I have to be strong. 'I mean it, Noah,' I whisper finally when he fails to answer. This is what I was afraid of. Noah's innate sense of decency won't allow him to sit on the sidelines when someone he cares about is suffering, but if he can't do as I ask, then it really is better to walk away now. We stare at each other, completely oblivious to Kit and Freddy sitting silently on the sofa opposite.

Then he shakes his head slowly, eyes still steady on mine. 'I don't know if I can do that, Tory,' he says at length. His voice is low but determined. 'How can I not get involved if I can help?'

'Ruining your career won't help anybody.' I force back the tears, wondering how we got to this so quickly, after all my efforts so far have failed to budge him an inch. My heart is thudding in a staccato rhythm, so hard I'm sure they can all hear it. 'Your agent said exactly the same thing,' I continue fiercely, ignoring his dismissive scowl as I throw his agent's words back in his face again. 'Tim understands that everything you've worked for is teetering on a knife edge.'

'Do you think any of that matters?' he snaps back heatedly, finally losing his patience. 'How many times and in how many ways can I say this. You are more important to me than my acting career. I can't sit back and watch the woman I love go through hell without trying to do something about it.'

'How can you say that?' I burst out wretchedly, 'You won't feel that way when all your fans have turned away from you; when the movie roles stop coming and you're reduced to advertising cleaning products on a cable channel.' I stop, unable to go on, my anger and misery hanging in the air like a physical thing.

At my outburst, Noah simply stares at me before closing his eyes and shaking his head wearily. When he finally opens them, I can see his withdrawal in their beautiful depths. 'Don't do this, Tory, please don't do this,' he warns in a low voice, but I have no answer. The lump in my throat is the size of a boulder, and I squeeze my eyes shut, trying to force back tears. When I finally manage to speak, my voice feels like it belongs to someone else.

'I don't want your help, Noah. We've got this, my dad and I.'

'So, we can only stay together if I sit on the sidelines like your bitch, is that it?' His voice as he lashes out is scathing, and my heart feels like it's breaking. 'Are we a partnership, Tory?' he continues angrily. 'Have we ever truly been a couple? Or am I just your pinup, like something out of a magazine, someone to sigh over - a nice daydream, but not real, not really part of your life?'

'No, it's not like that,' I cry, making no more effort to stem the tears flowing down my cheeks. 'I just don't want you to lose your career.'

'That's my choice to make,' he retorts vehemently. 'If my so-called fans turn away and the movie roles dry up, I can live with that. But you can't can you, Tory? It doesn't fit in with the fairy tale.' He pauses and runs his hand through his hair with a small, frustrated groan, before continuing in a softer tone, 'Can't you see, Tory, I'm a normal flesh and blood man, not just some idol to be pinned on someone's wall.' Then, achingly, 'Ask for my help, as your lover and your partner. Ask me to support you. I'm me, Noah – you *know* me, Tory.'

I stare helplessly at him, my whole body a maelstrom of heartache and grief. 'I... I can't, I just can't let you lose everything because of me,' I sob finally and watch him close his eyes and slump in defeat.

At length, climbing wearily to his feet, he says flatly, 'I wouldn't have lost everything, I'd still have the thing that matters most. But this isn't about me, Tory. This is about you. You're simply too afraid people will look at you and say, 'Bloody hell, he gave up fame and fortune for *her*?" He emphasises the word *her*, pouring scorn and disbelief into one word. 'You just don't understand that all of that Hollywood stuff – it's not real. What we had – me and you – *that* was real.' I have time to note that he's speaking about our relationship in the past tense, then he turns and walks towards the stairs without looking back.

It's five o'clock. Noah's been gone for exactly four hours, thirteen minutes and twenty-six seconds. I'm sitting alone in the Great Hall and feel as though someone has taken a sledgehammer to my heart. The worst thing is the fear that it's all my fault – that I've brought this misery on myself.

Kit, Freddy and Mabel are upstairs packing. I can't face my bedroom at the moment – it smells too much of Noah. So here I am, feeling miserable and wretched with the two dogs my only companions. Dotty is curled up on my knee, licking my hand in silent commiseration every few minutes, and Pickles is on the floor with his head resting on my foot. Even Spike, who's made himself scarce since the curtain episode, is sitting on top of the dining table, watching me unblinkingly. Animals are more sympathetic than humans sometimes. Not that my friends haven't shown compassion, but it's clear they think I fell out of the stupid tree and hit every branch on the way down.

I didn't see Noah after he went up to our bedroom, instead, I mumbled my apologies to Kit and Freddy, and simply left, walking until I couldn't see the Tower anymore. Then, collapsing onto the hard ground, I buried my head into my hands and wept, both dogs licking anxiously at the salty water as it dripped off my nose.

By the time Kit and Freddy turned up about twenty minutes later to sit on the grass beside me, the tears had finally dried up, leaving me feeling like a wizened old prune. Looking up, I saw in their eyes that Noah had gone. Wordlessly, they both put an arm around me, and we sat huddled together in silence. There really wasn't anything to say. After a while though, I gently extracted myself and said, 'Let's go home.'

Stroking Dotty absently, I come back to the present and look around at the beautiful, faded furnishings in the Great Hall. Fittingly the weather has been overcast today, so there's no sun shining to soften the decay, causing the room to look disturbingly like Miss Haversham's house in Great Expectations.

Shivering slightly, I make a move to go upstairs to pack, but, as I put Dotty on the floor, Aileen bustles in with tea and shortbread. I open my mouth to say I'm not hungry but suddenly realize I haven't actually eaten anything today and I'm ravenous. She places the tray onto the coffee table and hovers, clearly wanting to say something, and I look up at her expectantly as I take a bite of her delicious homemade shortbread. To my surprise, she sits herself down beside me and places a warm hand on my shoulder. 'It's gaein be awricht ance the pain has gane awa,' she murmurs, and for the first time since we've been here, I understand exactly what she's trying to say.

Chapter Twelve

The train to London was late getting into Paddington, and Jimmy found himself anxiously tearing up the pieces of his paper coffee cup as he stared unseeing out of the window.

He'd received a brief phone call from the Admiral at five o'clock this morning asking Jimmy to meet him in London pronto. Obligingly, the small man had immediately dropped everything, making the excuse to his wife that he was going fishing. Had he not been so worried, he might have picked a better reason for his absence, since he'd never actually been fishing before in his life. But perhaps Emily knew him better than he thought, as she'd taken one look at his anxious face before saying mildly, 'Try not to get yourself into any trouble love and let me know when you're on your way home.' He hoped he wouldn't have to break his promise about staying away from trouble. His track record where the Admiral was concerned certainly wasn't encouraging.

As the train finally pulled into Paddington Station, Jimmy quickly texted the Admiral's phone as instructed, and after a couple of fretful minutes, he received a reply telling him to make his way to a café in Pimlico. Forty-five minutes later, he was pushing open the door to a tiny eatery tucked away in a forgotten corner just off Regency Street. Looking around the small airless dining room, Jimmy thought for a second he'd come to the wrong place, then he spied two men sitting in the corner, and although he couldn't quite make out the one with his back to him, the other portly gentleman, sitting next to the window and wearing a ridiculous straw hat was unmistakably Charles Shackleford. Hurriedly, Jimmy made his way over, saying breathlessly as he reached the table, 'I'm so glad I've found you, Sir. I was really beginning to get worried.'

In time honoured tradition, the Admiral's response was to look up at Jimmy irritably before saying, 'Bloody hell, Jimmy, you trying to get the attention of the whole bollocking café? Stop making a spectacle and sit yourself down.' Jimmy opened his mouth to argue that his entrance could hardly be described as a spectacle, but before he could speak, he glanced down at the Admiral's companion, and the words died in his throat.

Hugo Buchannan. He hadn't seen the Scotsman for nearly forty years, but in that instant, it was as though those years had never existed and Jimmy was transported back to a dingy alley in Bangkok. Squeezing himself into the corner of the small table, Jimmy felt his apprehension rise. He really didn't know what to say, so he simply nodded to Hugo and mumbled a hasty greeting.

The Admiral didn't seem to pick up on Jimmy's anxiety, which wasn't really surprising as Charles Shackleford was normally about as intuitive as a sack of potatoes. Instead, after informing them both that he intended to order some scran before they got down to business, the Admiral waved over the waitress, and arbitrarily ordered for all three of them. 'I don't like tuna,' was all Hugo Buchannan said when the waitress disappeared into the kitchen, to which the Admiral's only response was a puzzled look as if to ask what his point was. Then, shifting himself forward in his chair, the Admiral leaned forward, looked at Jimmy and Hugo in turn and said in a low voice, 'I've come up with a plan...'

We decide to start out immediately after dinner, taking it in turns to drive through the night. As we leave, Aileen hugs each of us in turn before plying us with lots of goodies to eat on the journey so the only stops we'll need to make are for petrol and weak bladders. There's still no sign of old Mrs. Buchannan and thinking back to my last little chat with Jason, I really do hope she's not actually popped her clogs. Still, Aileen doesn't look particularly worried, and she knows her better than we do.

I stand a few yards away from the car, giving the dogs a last chance to do their business while watching Freddy load the suitcases into the boot. I have no idea where I'm going to stay when we get back to Dartmouth. The Admiralty will likely still be swarming with journalists, but it's enough that I'm going back to familiar turf. Maybe then, somehow, I can let Noah go, and focus on what's going to happen to my father.

Doggy business taken care of, I walk back towards the car, to see Mabel clambering laboriously into the back, all the while thanking Aileen effusively for her delightful "vittles" (she's definitely been with my father too long...) Within ten minutes of us starting out, she's snoring in time with the dogs. Freddy drew the short straw for the first stint in the back and has Mabel's head on one shoulder, Pickles's head on the other and Dotty on his lap. 'Are we there yet?' he mutters plaintively as Mabel lets out a particularly loud snore directly in his ear. Kit and I laugh – it's the first one I've cracked today, and it actually feels good.

We finally arrive in Devon just after seven am. The journey was long but uneventful for which I'm profoundly grateful. The drama over the last few days would keep *East Enders* going for the next ten years. Despite my friends' willingness to alternate, I did most of the driving. At the moment, I'm not sure I'll ever sleep again. As I pull into the motorway services just outside Exeter, I wake up the others so we can freshen ourselves up a bit before coming up with some kind of plan as to exactly what we're going to do with me when we hit the bright lights of Dartmouth. We take turns to use the loo, then hole up in the car with hot coffee and good old McDonalds McMuffins all round. By the time we finish, the inside smells of fuggy dog and hamburger.

Kit offers to let me stay at her place again, but her flat is in the middle of the town. With the Regatta only a week away, Dartmouth is likely to be heaving with tourists, and until the press get bored and move onto the next story, I don't want to risk her flat being blockaded by hordes of prying journalists and spectators. I need somewhere quiet where I can focus on helping my father get his name cleared, but close enough to my friends so that they can actually get on with their lives while they're propping me up. I know I'm selfish to expect them to continue with the whole moral support thing, but the truth is, I don't think I can get through this without them. Weak – who me?

We sit chewing our thumbs. Mabel offers to let me come to hers, but quite frankly she's got enough with Pickles, and, on the off chance that my father's released any time soon, she might well be looking after him as well, at least for a while. Of course, if she does, it will no doubt show her whether she's actually ready to take on the unpredictable oddball that is my dad...

In the end, Kit comes up with an idea that everyone seems to think is cracking apart from me. Ben Sheppherd's yacht. When she first mentions it, I look at her as though she's lost the plot. 'It's hardly a gin palace,' I say eventually, only to be put back in my box with Freddie's, 'Well, sweetie, I hate to say this to you, but beggars can't be choosers.'

'He's not sailing in the Regatta this year,' continues Kit, completely ignoring my less than enthusiastic response to her suggestion. 'His boat is moored up on a buoy in the middle of the Dart. No one's likely to spot you there.'

No one's likely to spot me ever again,' I argue as they all nod their heads eagerly. 'How am I going to get off the bloody thing?'

'Row,' say Kit and Freddy in unison. As I stare at them appalled, Freddy callously adds, 'It will help with your weight, sweetie.'

'You're such a bitch,' I grumble as Kit hurriedly takes out her mobile phone. 'I notice you've not offered your flat as a refuge. Some friend you are.' I know I'm being petulant, but, come on, a *boat*? And not the sort that's likely to be moored up in Monte Carlo, or even the Dart Marina.

'God no, darling,' he responds with a theatrical shudder. 'Couldn't possibly have your smalls hanging up in my bathroom. However, fear not sweet friend, I will row to you daily with supplies, so you don't starve.' I snort inelegantly. The last time Freddy rowed anywhere was in secondary school when he decided to take up canoeing because someone told him it would improve his arm muscles. As I recall, he lasted two lessons before he capsized and had to be resuscitated by the instructor – an Amazon of a woman with as much hair on her top lip as Dotty. Freddy credits her with his decision to bat for the other side.

Kit waves at us both to shut up as she begins speaking, and I sigh, realizing there's no stopping this runaway train. The only thing I can hope for is that Ben's changed his mind about sailing. A minute later, that last hope is dashed as Kit gives a thumbs-up. 'Ben, you're an absolute star,' she enthuses. 'I'll call you again as we get into Dartmouth.'

'I take it that's a yes,' I grouch as she finishes the call, and she nods her head with a big smile. 'Yep, it's all sorted. I told him I'd fill him in when we see him, but of course he's seen the news. Says he's happy to help. He's a good guy, Tory, you know that, and he's not a blabbermouth. He'll keep it to himself.'

'Well, that's that then,' I gripe, unwilling to let my sulk go just yet (even though absolutely no one's paying any attention), 'Come on, Dotty, we'll let one of these bossy so-called friends drive while we cuddle up and Google ways of combatting sea sickness.'

I open the door to get into the back while my supposed BFFs simply choose to ignore my pain and laugh heartlessly.

We arrive in Dartmouth at the worst possible time. There are so many people, it proves impossible to park anywhere near the boat float. After driving round for ten minutes, we give up and head back to Kit's rented garage which actually costs her nearly as much as her flat. Sitting in the gloom, we debate what to do next. 'Look, I'll just put on some dark glasses and a hat, it's not like people are out looking for me like they are Noah.' It hurts so much to say his name, and talking about disguises brings back even more memories. I swallow the lump that suddenly appears in my throat as Kit touches my arm in sympathy, well aware of my wobble.

In the end, we agree that Freddy will escort Mabel and Pickles over to Kingswear on the passenger ferry, while Kit and I both don suitable camouflage (after all it's common knowledge to everyone who lives in Dartmouth that she's my best friend) and walk down to meet Ben Sheppherd at the boat float. We agree to rendezvous at five in my new temporary floating home, at which time Kit and Freddy will bring supplies.

As she leaves, I give Mabel a big hug, surprised at the depth of affection I feel for the elderly matron. 'I'll give you a call later to let you know any developments,' I say before bending down to give Pickles a quick fuss and instructing him to be good for Aunty Mabel.

'Try not to worry too much about your dad, Tory,' she responds, taking hold of Pickles's lead and following Freddy out of the garage, 'He really is a tough old boot.'

I can't help but smile at her accurate assessment of my father, and I suddenly realize that Mabel is exactly the right person to take my irascible parent in hand – providing he doesn't end up in a Thai jail...

Ben is waiting for us when we finally arrive at the river and doesn't waste any time chatting. He gives me enough time to give Kit a quick kiss and a hug goodbye before guiding me quickly to his waiting dinghy - mercifully complete with small motor. I'm beginning to think I should be wearing Dior sunglasses and a silk headscarf – sort of a la Grace Kelly – to take full advantage of my situation. Still, maybe not. No one is taking the slightest notice of my current less-than-elegant attire. Once I'm seated, he hands Dotty to me, and she sits shivering as we head out into the middle of the Dart. It only takes us a couple of minutes to reach our destination, and I just have time to register *small*, before Ben is steadying the dinghy against the ladder and shoving me unceremoniously up onto the deck. Next, he passes me my trembling dog and then, after securing the dinghy, quickly shins up the ladder with my small suitcase.

As he shows me around Dartmouth Belle, I can sense how proud he is, and if I'm being honest, it is rather charming in a 'let's go sailing for a couple of hours' kind of way, but by the time he's explained how to use the composting toilet, some of the appeal has most definitely been lost. You may be wondering how someone who has lived by the river all her life could be so negative about boats. The truth is, I'm not really. I love sailing, as long as someone else is doing the pulling and hauling, but, unlike Kit, I've never actually spent the night on anything afloat. Obviously, this will be something I can brag about to my best friend after all this is over – yay, go me...

After giving me instructions on how to use the small calor gas stove, Ben tells me to make myself comfortable in the tiny saloon, and things start to look up as he lifts a cushion and reaches into a miniscule fridge. Small it might be, but it's big enough to hold a bottle of wine. 'Thought you might need this,' he says with a small sympathetic grin, earning my undying gratitude. There are even plastic wine glasses, and as he pours a generous measure of rosé in each, it all suddenly seems a bit more like a fun adventure. Until he speaks. 'You going to tell me what's going on, Tory?' he asks softly, making it clear that it's my choice. I look over my wine glass at him and wonder how I never noticed that he's actually quite attractive in a quiet unassuming way. I recall what Kit said about his marriage falling apart. I'm not the only one with a broken heart it seems. I take a large sip of my wine and stroke Dotty who is currently doing her best to be surgically grafted to my lap, then I take a deep breath and tell him everything.

It's actually five thirty before Ben gets a call from Kit to tell him she and Freddy are at the boat float, and as he goes off to collect them, I lean back and close my eyes. I'm finding it difficult to think straight – I suppose being awake for over twenty-four hours can do that to you. I know I need to talk to my father. He obviously still thinks we're in Scotland, and I'm wondering if he's using the lack of a signal at Bloodstone Tower to avoid calling me. The problem is I don't actually have any idea where he is. I rub my head in weary frustration. I haven't got Hugo or Jason's mobile numbers either, what a numpty. Still, maybe Jimmy's heard something. I resolve to call him the minute I can gather the strength to get my phone out of my pocket...

I wake to the sound of voices and slamming of cupboards. 'Ah, sleeping beauty awakes,' definitely comes from Freddy. I blink and look down at Dotty who is still sitting snuggled up on my lap. It's not like her to miss the opportunity of a frenzied barking session to say hello. Maybe she's knackered too – although recalling her almost constant snoring on the journey down, I find that hard to believe. I stroke her head softly thinking it's more likely she's too scared to get off my knee. I hope she manages to shake off her fear soon or getting her to do her business is likely to prove a bit of a challenge.

'Are you hungry?' Kit this time. I look up realizing I'm famished. 'What have you brought?' I lean forward to have a look but stay seated. The tiny galley is crowded with one and positively rammed with two. Add to that the fact that Freddy is struggling to uncork something alcoholic, and at any moment could well be giving Kit an impromptu lobotomy, I wisely decide to stay put.

'I've got a large French stick,' she says waving it at me as though I might just miss the three-foot-long loaf, 'And to go with it, cheese, ham, pâté and olives. There wasn't a massive amount of choice for a Monday afternoon, M&S had practically been cleaned out by ravenous tourists.'

'Mmm, that sounds lovely.' My voice must have sounded pretty eager, so Kit throws me a piece of baguette, which I endeavour to snatch out of the air before Dotty manages to get there first. The little dog is now sitting up looking much more alert. There's nothing like food to bring her round. I tear apart the wonderfully fresh bread with my teeth without sparing a bit for Dotty who's now looking at me as though I'm a cross between Cruella Deville and Lucrezia Borgia.

'Where's Ben?' I ask, finally noting there are only three of us. 'Said he had things to do,' Kit responds, popping an olive into her mouth. 'I think he was really giving us some privacy. Nice guy. Said he'd swing by later to pick us up.' I nod my head, my mouth busy making short work of the crust.

'Have you spoken to your parents, Kit?' I ask after finally managing to swallow. I'm very aware that I've been so consumed with my own problems over the last few days that I've given hardly any thought to what Kit must be going through at the thought of losing her beloved gallery. Seeing I've finished, she throws another piece of bread at me before answering – I'm beginning to feel like a performing seal.

'They've left a couple of messages. They're intending to come back to Dartmouth in late September to put it on the market. Apparently, what it fetches will keep them in cruises for the next ten years.' I really don't know what to say. I hardly know Kit's parents. She was left in the care of her aunt Florence once she reached puberty, while they went abroad. The gallery is the last of their property sold to fund an obsession with travelling. 'They say it's time for me to get a real job, that they can't support me in my little hobby any longer.'

'That's ridiculous,' I burst out. 'They can't really believe that. You've put your heart and soul into that gallery.' Freddy hands me a glass of fizz.

'The problem is darling that property fetches so much in Dartmouth now, and Kit's parents are obviously running out of the readies.'

'Let's not talk about it anymore,' Kit responds as I open my mouth to speak again. 'Everything happens for a reason. Maybe I'm ready for another challenge. And, anyway, we've got more pressing problems than my employment situation. Shall we eat up top?' She hands the food tray to Freddy before making her way resolutely up the stairs to the deck, clearly wanting to put an end to the conversation. I sigh, knowing of old that when Kit doesn't want to talk, she simply won't. Leaning back down, she reaches for the tray held up in Freddy's hands with instructions for him to bring the wine. And that is pretty much that.

We sit in the little cockpit with our tray of goodies resting on a lifebuoy. The early evening weather is sunny and humid, the sort that promises an awesome thunderstorm later. As I take another sip of my sparkling wine, I look out over the river, still bustling with yachts and boats of all sizes, and hear the sound of muted laughter drifting over the water. I don't think I've ever felt quite so isolated from the rest of the world, and I ruthlessly shove down the thought of being here with Noah – just the two of us. God, I miss him so much. I wonder where he is now, and unable to help myself, I twist round to look towards the mouth of the Dart. To my relief, his house is hidden from view.

'He's in Ireland,' responds Kit quietly to my wistful look. 'That's where he said he was going anyway. I think they're going to be filming there.' I turn back to look at my two friends, both regarding me sympathetically. But there really is nothing else to say. Instead, I reach down to help myself to some bread and pâté, giving some to Dotty who finally appears to have gotten over her fear of boats, or at least put it aside in favour of her stomach.

'I think the best thing to do for starters is to call Jimmy,' I say with false optimism. 'He could well have more information about Dad's whereabouts.' Then, determined to focus on something, anything to stop me thinking about what I've lost, I fish around for my mobile phone and bring up Jimmy's number. He answers on the second ring, leading me to think he's been waiting for my call.

'Tory?' His voice is filled with relief.

'Have you heard from Dad?' I say without preamble.

'I spoke to him this morning,' Jimmy answers, equally happy not to waste time in small talk. 'Told me to give you the message that you're not to worry, everything's being sorted out. He's positive all the charges will be dropped. You're to give him a couple of days, then he'll call you.'

'Here we go again, don't worry, Tory, stop fussing, Tory, trust me, Tory.' My voice is loud as I feel the frustrated anger begin to swamp me. 'When for fuck's sake is somebody going to tell me the truth?' There's a shocked silence on the other end of the line. I don't swear often, and definitely not to Jimmy who's been like a second father to me my whole life. 'I'm sorry, Jimmy,' I mumble eventually, my anger deflating like a popped balloon, 'I know you're protecting my father, but for pity's sake, the whole thing is beginning to wear bloody thin.'

'I know,' is his quiet answer. Then, after a short pause, 'Where are you? How are things with Noah?'

'Noah and I aren't together anymore. I'm okay. You don't have to worry about me. If you speak to Dad, tell him that he'd better damn well call me soon, or I'm coming to London myself to get some bloody answers.' Then I determinedly cut the call and shove my phone back into my pocket before saying brightly, 'Come on, Freddy, you're slacking. My glass has been empty for all of five minutes.'

By the time Ben comes to pick Kit and Freddy up just after nine, we are all more than a little squiffy. As they leave, I throw my arms around Kit, declaring that she's the best friend in the whole wide world. I want so badly to ask her to stay, but even in my slightly inebriated state, I know that she can't babysit me twenty-four seven. She needs some alone time to sort out her own life. And Freddy? Truth is, I'd probably end up shoving him overboard.

Instead, I stand on the deck and wave, watching them go, until their dots climb out of the dinghy at the boat float and finally disappear up the gang plank, swallowed up in the dusk. Then, I pick Dotty up and take her to do her business at the forward end of the yacht, which is where Ben says he's trained his dog to do it, and no doubt inspired by the leftover doggy smells, she obligingly squats down. After praising her effusively, I swill the deck as instructed and, taking her back down into the cabin, snuggle her little warm body to me, murmuring, 'We'll make a sailor of you yet, Dotspot.' Then I close the hatch, shutting out the world, take off my jeans and we both snuggle up under the slightly damp and salty duvet already made up in the tiny forward cabin.

Chapter Thirteen

Forty years ago…

'What the bloody hell do you mean, it's got your real name on it? Who the bollocking hell are you anyway?'

'I can't tell you.' Doris's voice came out in little more than a whisper. His face was white and strained, a stark contrast to the leftover streaks of blood now drying on his chin. Nervously, he twisted the ends of the remaining tissues in his hand. 'It's much better if you don't know, trust me.' He sighed as the two lieutenants remained silent, identical sceptical expressions on their faces. Then he continued frustratedly, 'It doesn't really matter who I am. The thing is, someone at that brothel might recognize the name, and if they do, then we're all done for.'

Charles snorted in derision before saying sarcastically, 'You can't be that bloody famous, sunshine. If we don't know who you are, I'm damn sure a Thai prostitute isn't going to cotton on. I don't think any of 'em spoke English anyway.'

'Can't you see, it's not me, it's the *name*,' Doris burst out, staring wildly at each officer. 'We have to get it back, we *have to*.' His urgency finally seemed to penetrate.

The two lieutenants glanced at each other before Hugo said, 'They've probably found it by now anyway, so this is all a bit like shutting the gate after the horse has bolted, so to speak.'

'No, no. The thing is, unlike my wallet, I hid it,' Doris continued, shaking his head. 'By the time I got into that room, my instincts were telling me I'd made a mistake...'

'From what I've seen, you've got the instincts of a bloody pot plant,' interrupted Charles testily, before impatiently waving the sub lieutenant to continue. 'There was a crack in the floorboards. I... I shoved the passport down there.'

Hugo frowned. 'How do you know she, I mean he, didn't see you do it?'

'Err - the err, person, was lighting some candles at the time.'

'Very bloody romantic. God you are such a complete knob jockey, Doris.' Charles sighed and looked over at Hugo. 'What do you think, Scotty? You believe this pile of codswallop?'

'What exactly do you think will happen if they do find out your name?' Hugo looked back at Doris without answering Charles.

There was a short pause as Doris evidently tried to choose his words carefully. Then, seemingly deciding that it was all or nothing, he finally raised his chin defiantly. 'Well, I'm so sorry to have to tell you this, Sir, but you, Lieutenant Shackleford and Able seaman Noon will very likely be court marshalled for starters. You could end up doing time in the slammer.' In the silence that followed, he lost his brief bravado, his voice wobbling as he said, 'Please Sirs, you have to help me. I know I've been a fool. I swear I don't know what I was thinking...'

'Thinking? You've done precious bloody little of that, Doris.' Charles's words were low and furious, causing the sub lieutenant to wince and drop his eyes. 'You've landed us all up bollocking shit creek. By rights, we should just turn this over to the Captain and be done with it, except, as you so eloquently put it, we could end up in bloody prison. Not you, I note - even though you're the biggest dipstick this side of the Suez – us.'

He paused, trying to take in the enormity of the mess they were in, then turned to Hugo, sitting in ashen silence on his bunk. 'We can't waste any time. If this bloody passport is as important as shit for brains here seems to think, we have to get it back before anyone has a chance to find it. Soon as our watch is over, we'll go ashore. We'll aim to be off the ship by seventeen hundred.' Then, turning to Doris, 'Go and find AB Noon and tell him I want to see him pronto. When are you on watch? On second thoughts, don't tell me, I'm not bloody interested. Whatever the watch bill is, if your stint clashes, get out of it. Use your *connections*.' Charles almost spat the last word, and Doris simply nodded, the expression on his face alternating between relief and terror.

'Yes Sir,' he mumbled at length when it appeared his superior had nothing else to say, and, after saluting clumsily, he excused himself and hastily left the room.

At just after a quarter past five, Charles, Hugo, Doris and Jimmy gathered at a local bar to discuss their strategy. Charles was the unelected leader of the mission, and he wasted no time in niceties. 'Has Hugo briefed you, Jimmy?' he asked, nodding quickly at Jimmy's mumbled assent. 'Okay. We've got five and a half hours to do this. If we're not back onboard by twenty-two hundred, at the start of the next watch, we're all up the swanny.

'Now the fewer that know about this bloody cake and arse party, the better, so that means we can't ask Kulap to take us. I don't want to advertise our presence by grabbing a ride, so that leaves walking, but it should take us no longer than half an hour if we leg it quick. Once we get there, we'll check the lay of the land, see how busy the place is. It's still pretty early, so I'm hoping it's going to be fairly quiet. Closed would be even better.

'We obviously can't just walk through the front door after the way we said our goodbyes last time, so first things first, we'll do a recce to locate the room the passport was left in, so we can plan our next move. Is that clear to everyone?' After making sure he received a nod from each solemn face individually, he pushed back his chair, saying, 'Right then, let's do this.'

In the end it was nearly an hour before they finally arrived at the dingy entrance to the so-called steamy shower massage parlour, the warren of lanes and alleys proving more difficult to navigate than they remembered. The flashing light above the door was turned off, and Charles was hoping that meant that it was still too early for anyone to be indulging in anything hot and steamy – shower or otherwise. Standing huddled in a doorway, the four men stood and surveyed the deserted scene in silence.

'Was the room on the front or the back?' Hugo whispered at length. 'Back, I think,' responded Doris. 'I remember briefly looking out of the window before I – I, er started get…'

'We get the picture,' Charles interrupted irritably, 'Exactly what did you see when you had a shufti?'

'Just a narrow alley with lots of crap around.'

'Very helpful,' was Charles's tense response. 'Jimmy, you're the smallest out of us, and, don't take this the wrong way, but you're the one who looks most like a native – you know black hair and the like.' The last bit was added in response to Jimmy's initial indignant expression. Charles didn't want any mutiny at this late stage. An argument in this neighbourhood was not likely to add anything positive to the situation, and he couldn't afford to risk Doris if the bloody idiot was as important as he claimed. Luckily, Jimmy knew his place, and, after a deep breath, he slipped out of the shelter and quickly disappeared round the side of the building.

The other three waited for what was probably only about five minutes but felt like forever. As Jimmy finally reappeared, Charles breathed a sigh of relief before whispering heatedly, 'Where the bloody hell have you been? I was about to send out Doris here to find you.' He ignored Doris's alarmed look and focused his attention on the nervously panting man in front of him.

'I think I found the alley,' Jimmy whispered urgently, 'But we need to get going quick. There's a window open on the ground floor. Think it might be a kitchen – smelt like it anyway. I had a quick shufti, and there was no one inside.'

'Right then, lead on.' Charles wasted no time and shoved the small man unceremoniously back in the direction he'd come from.

'Watch your step,' Jimmy called softly as he turned into a dark dingy, not to mention very smelly, passageway, 'There's some pretty nasty bits and pieces underfoot.' The faint swearing coming from behind him indicated that at least one of them had missed the warning and trodden in something revolting.

A minute or so later they emerged into a slightly wider alley. Although the smell didn't improve any, the sliver of sunlight penetrating between the dilapidated buildings made the going a little less treacherous. Jimmy hurried to the left without waiting to see if they followed, finally stopping about twenty yards away just before an open window. 'You sure this is the place?' Hugo muttered as they caught up with him. 'I reckon,' Jimmy responded with a shrug. 'Only one way to find out anyway.'

'But what if you're wrong?' came Doris's heated undertone.

Jimmy waved his hand towards the remainder of the alley before answering, 'There's nothing after this, I had a look – they're all warehouses and stuff. No one's lived in 'em for donkey's years.'

'Enough,' Charles held up his hand to put a stop to the whispered bickering. 'Here's what we're going to do.

'I'll go first, then Jimmy and Doris. Scotty, you stay out here and watch for anyone dodgy.' He turned to Doris and laid his hand heavily on the sub lieutenant's shoulder. 'I need you to come with us 'cos you're the only one who knows exactly where you hid the bollocking passport. But put one step wrong Doris Day, and I swear I'll leave you here to face the music on your own.' Doris nodded, white faced, and satisfied the younger man understood it was no bluff, Charles turned towards the open window and, as quietly as possible, heaved himself through.

A couple of minutes later the three of them were standing silently in the dim interior of the kitchen waiting tensely to see if they'd been rumbled. Charles couldn't help but notice the bloody bits and pieces of unrecognizable meat littering the counter – if nothing else, the smell would have alerted him, not to mention Doris's stifled retching beside him. 'You're such a bloody pansy,' the lieutenant muttered, tiptoeing towards the door. Opening it quietly, he peered out into a corridor, turning back to his companions after a second to whisper, 'We're in the right place. Follow behind me, and for God's sake keep the noise down. Jimmy, you take up the rear.'

The three of them crept softly along the passage towards a set of stairs. Unfortunately, they weren't the same ones they'd crashed down so publicly on their last visit, so once they got to the top, they had to stop to get their bearings. Charles held up his hand for quiet, studying each of the doors in turn. Suddenly, the sound of voices came from the other end of the corridor, and they shrank back against the wall as a door opened to reveal a man being shoved unceremoniously out of a room, still doing up his trousers.

The tirade coming from inside the room was shrill, and in answer, they heard heavy footsteps coming from the opposite direction, finally disclosing a large mean looking man with a scar running down one side of his face. Without ceremony, the thug grabbed hold of the unfortunate man and dragged him yelling and shouting along the corridor and down the main stairs. The three winced and looked at each other as the bellowing abruptly stopped.

'Shit,' muttered Doris, looking for a second as if he were about to bolt. Sensing his panic, Charles grabbed hold of the sub lieutenant's collar and held him still.

'He's done us a favour,' the lieutenant whispered to his two companions, purposely shying away from thinking about the possible fate of the unlucky stranger. 'I can tell where we are now. Follow me.' He waited for another couple of seconds to make sure Doris had calmed down, then moved stealthily down the corridor towards a door on the right. 'This is the one,' he murmured without looking back. Slowly, he eased the handle down and pushed the door ajar, waiting a few seconds to see if anyone inside the room called out. When they heard nothing, he cautiously put his head round the opening and looked into the bedroom. Relief swamped him when he saw it was empty. Beckoning the other two, he slipped inside and closed the door softly behind them.

Once inside the room, Doris didn't wait to be told and hurried towards the crack in the floorboard where he'd hidden his passport. After a couple of tense seconds, his face cracked into a triumphant smile as his fingers found what they were searching for. Waving his prize in the air, he climbed to his feet and stepped forward, directly onto the same crack. With an ominous splintering sound, the wood disintegrated, and his foot disappeared into the jagged opening.

For a second, the three men stood stock still. Just as they thought the noise had gone unnoticed, they heard shouting, followed by the unmistakable sounds of feet running up the stairs. 'Bollocks,' muttered Charles, hurrying to lock the bedroom door.

'What are we going to do?' hissed Doris, glancing wildly between Charles and Jimmy as the footsteps got louder.

'Well, there's no way out the way we came, that's for sure. See if you can open that window, Jimmy.' The small man dashed to the window without argument, and straining, pulled at the grimy frame. 'Here, give us a hand, Doris,' he yelled, stealth obviously no longer an issue. Shoving the passport into his pocket, Doris rushed to help, and the two men slowly began to slide the window upwards, just as someone began rattling the door handle.

Charles wasted no time waiting to see if they managed to get the window open, smashing it would do equally well if necessary. Instead, he grabbed the sheets off the bed and quickly knotted the two together. Glancing towards the door, he registered that whoever was on the other side had now resorted to kicking it. They had a few seconds at most.

Urgently he tied one end onto the bedstead, pulling at the knot experimentally to see if it would hold, then he tossed the other end to Jimmy who quickly launched the fabric out of the now open window. He briefly saw Hugo's white face staring up at him anxiously, then Jimmy was climbing over the sill and lowering himself down the makeshift rope.

Once on the ground, he called up to Doris, 'Your turn mate.' For a second Doris's face disappeared then re-emerged as he was shoved unceremoniously out of the opening, for a moment almost hanging in midair, until his survival instincts kicked in, and he slid clumsily down the sheet. Before he reached the bottom, Charles was climbing over the sill, only narrowly avoiding an arm as it lunged out of the window to grab him.

'Go,' yelled the lieutenant as he hit the ground, pushing the other three towards the dingy passageway. He was just about to follow, when he heard an ominous ripping sound and, looking up, he saw the same scar-faced man hanging with one hand on the sheet which was slowly tearing apart. Unable to move, Charles stared up as the man, who was now shouting desperately, began to slide towards the ground, almost in slow motion. Suddenly, the sheet gave way and the man plummeted to the ground, landing with a dull thud.

For a second Charles stood paralyzed, then, as he saw the man move, slowly trying to lever himself off the ground, he instinctively went towards him to see if he could help. As he bent down, the man groaned and flopped onto his back, revealing a large knife sticking out of his chest. Charles recalled the thug stalking towards him back in the bedroom, brandishing a large knife, and he realized the man had fallen onto his own blade.

Hearing a noise behind him, he spun round, only to see his three companions, still standing immobile at the narrow entrance to the passageway. 'What the bloody hell are you doing?' he hissed. 'Get your arses out of here.' Then he turned back to the groaning man, unwilling to leave without trying to help somehow. The blood stain had now spread over the whole of the man's shirt and Charles grabbed at the fallen sheet in a futile effort to try and stop the bleeding.

All of a sudden there was a shriek from the recently vacated window and the lieutenant looked up to see a woman leaning out of the window screaming gibberish at the top of her voice. Heart thumping, he looked back down to the man on the ground, only to see his eyes wide open unseeing towards the sky. Realizing there was nothing more he could do, Charles glanced up briefly once more, but as the woman's screeching reached a crescendo, he did the only thing left to him to do. He scarpered.

The four conspirators waited anxiously for the next few days to see if there were going to be any repercussions. Under Charles's orders, they stayed on board and avoided spending any time together until the ship finally sailed two weeks later. Once at sea, they finally relaxed a little, vowing to keep what happened strictly between the four of them. Doris was transferred from Hermes when they reached Hong Kong.

The other three never found out what his real name was because they never saw him again.

Chapter Fourteen

It's three o'clock in the morning and, lying in my little bunk, I don't think I've ever been so scared in my life. I know Dotty hasn't – she's currently under the covers, curled up and whimpering between my legs. The threatened storm started just after midnight, and since then, I've been lying here, feeling the small yacht roll and pitch violently, every toss threatening to bring up the bread, cheese and pâté I consumed earlier. As I listen to the rigging clashing and banging against the mast, I actually begin to wonder if I should have made a will.

To try and keep myself occupied I decide who I should leave my possessions to. Kit and Freddy of course – I don't think my dad totally appreciates my taste. I wonder if there's a pen and paper in any of the cupboards so I can write my wishes down – still, I suppose if the yacht goes down, my wishes will go down with it. I get as far as planning mine and Dotty's funeral – of course we'll want to go together.

I picture the mourners sobbing as the open casket is brought into the church with me lying pale and ethereal (where did that come from? I've never been remotely ethereal, or pale for that matter – still if my end's a watery one…) Back to my imaginings - hard to believe this is taking my mind off things, but actually, it is. Both Dotty and I look as though we're sleeping, and I picture Kit and Freddy propping up Noah, almost crazy with grief. My father is in the background shouting, 'Why, why?' with his hands raised to the heavens.

I'm so engrossed in my gruesome fantasy that I fail to notice the cupboard above my head come open after a particularly violent roll, until suddenly, shockingly a large hard object drops directly onto my head. I have time to utter a small 'oomph,' before something else falls out, this time breaking open en route and covering both me and the bed liberally with flour. I ask you – who the bloody hell has self-rising flour on a sodding boat?

Rearing up, I gasp, inadvertently inhaling half a pound of the white stuff which I then proceed to cough and choke up, all the while praying hysterically it is actually flour and not drugs. Eventually, the coughing subsides and luckily, I'm not seeing little green men, or mermaids, and certainly don't feel the urge to launch myself off the rigging.

Sighing in relief, I struggle out of bed (Dotty doesn't move) and, pulling open the cabin door, stagger over to the small sink, intending to at least wash the stuff off my face. Unfortunately, despite pumping my foot frantically, there doesn't seem to be any water, so I decide to open the hatch a little and hold out my cloth to let the rain do its stuff. Bracing myself against the stairs, I lean forward to unlock and push open the hatch with one hand, intending to hold out my cloth with the other. Unfortunately, the wind whips both hatch doors out of my grip, throwing them open with a crash, and a large deluge of water slaps me squarely in the face. Coughing and spluttering for the second time, I rear back, trying to shelter from the rain now driving directly into the cabin courtesy of the ten-force gale going on outside.

For a second, I stand immobile, trying to wipe the now floury white goo out of my eyes. Then it suddenly occurs to me that if too much water gets into the cabin, there's a chance we really could sink, and all of a sudden, my funeral plans don't seem quite so comforting. I know I have to do something, so taking a deep breath, I climb up the stairs, and lean out into the storm.

Trying to ignore the rain lashing across my face and head, I reach out to the handles of the hatch doors and slowly pull them towards me. After what seems like ages, they suddenly bang together and lock with a loud snap. Wearily, I sit down on the stairs and happen to catch sight of myself in a small mirror on the bulkhead. My head and shoulders are wet through and patchily covered in off-white gunk. If I had longer ears, I'd look like an extra out of *A Hundred and One Dalmatians*.

Grabbing a small towel off a hook next to the hatch, which I suspect may have been strategically placed to take care of impromptu soakings such as this, I wipe ineffectually at the sticky mess which, by the time daylight comes, will no doubt have dried to a nice hard crust. Resisting the urge to cry (seems to be what I do best at the moment), I give up wiping my face and rest my head in my hands.

After several minutes, I suddenly realize that the boat has stopped rocking and, looking up, I cock my head to listen. The wind has died down. Breathing another sigh of relief, I hang the now sticky towel back up and make my way back to my bunk. As I shut the cabin door behind me, I see Dotty's nose sticking out of the top of the duvet, her head resting comfortably on my pillow. Smiling, I get in beside her and, snuggling her up to my belly, I finally fall into a mercifully dreamless sleep.

Despite his reassurance to Tory the evening before, Jimmy wasn't at all sure that the Admiral's plan was going to go as smoothly as his former commanding officer seemed to think. However, he had to applaud the Admiral's foresight in keeping hold of the small Polaroid photograph taken of him and Doris in the red light district of Patpong in Bangkok, especially as the date was printed on the bottom right-hand corner.

Jimmy remembered it as though it was yesterday. The sightseeing tour that none of them wanted to go on apart from Sub Lieutenant Day, whose every whim was inexplicably pandered to by the Captain of HMS Hermes during their three-month deployment to Hong Kong. The outing that had ended so disastrously, he'd buried, but never forgotten it.

Sighing, Jimmy brought his mind back to the present. His job was to make sure that Tory didn't 'stick her nose in,' as the Admiral put it. All three of them had a copy of the photo, along with a letter, written by the Admiral, describing exactly the events of the fateful two days. Both he and Hugo were given instructions to keep both the letter and the photo hidden, 'just in case.'

The number of the safety deposit box containing the original snapshot was disguised on a postcard that had already been sent to their home addresses earlier. Jimmy privately thought that this was probably the weakest link in the Admiral's plan given the fact that should she get there first, Emily was very likely to either chuck away any correspondence sent from the Admiral or hand it in to the nearest police station... Still, he was keeping a close watch for the post and hopefully he'd get there in time to stash the card away without his wife spotting it.

Hugo's part of the plan was simply to march into the Home Office and threaten to make the photo public along with their story, while the Admiral handed himself in to the Metropolitan Police.

The biggest gamble of course was that none of them had the slightest clue who Doris really was, whether his family name really was as important as he'd seemed to think or whether the knobs in the British Government were likely to give a toss either way...

∞ ∞ ∞

I've now been stuck on this bloody boat for two whole days, and I really am slowly turning into Freddy's bag lady. Since coming on board, I've only managed to have a strip wash which has done nothing to remove the now grey dried on pancake mix that is determinedly clinging to my hair and chin. In fact, I'm beginning to think that nothing less than Swarfega oil and grease remover is going to get it off. I'm actually starting to look as though I have leprosy.

I haven't seen Kit and Freddy since Monday evening. I totally understand that they have their own lives to take care of, and I've taken up too much of their time recently, but it doesn't stop me feeling grouchy and unloved. Of course, being alone ensures that the one person I don't want to think about is totally dominating my thoughts. Plus, I'm running out of clothes, and asking Jimmy to pop over to the Admiralty to pick me up some more underwear is just way too creepy. He's been very patient with me though. I think on the whole I've been calling him every hour to ask if he's got an update. Every time we speak, he says to trust my dad and sit tight. Sometimes I can't help but wonder if my father's actually paying him.

The only plus side of the whole life on the ocean wave thing is that Dotty has now well and truly got her sea legs. In fact, she appears to love it on board. She spends all her time in between snacks sitting on the forward deck where she watches the river traffic, lifting her nose to the wind, obviously relishing the smells carried on the sea air. Not only that, but she has me all to herself. Always a bonus in Dotty's eyes.

My phone beeps and, as usual, my heart lifts briefly just on the off chance it's Noah. Of course, it isn't, but it is the next best person. Kit. She apologizes profusely for not coming over last night, bless her, but is bringing fish and chips over at six. Yay. I text back to say she's now my favourite person in the whole world and not to forget the salt and vinegar. Enough with the moping, I have knickers to rinse out...

It takes me half an hour to wash and peg out my underwear, which is now paraded prettily along the yacht railing, then it's back to brooding. Being a naturally enquiring person (Kit calls it nosy and always says I'd be in, if I fell in...), the lack of news is really beginning to grate. I know Jimmy's only trying to be kind, but I really need to know what's happening.

I sit in the cockpit, idly biting my fingernails. As I look down at their bitten ragged tips, I reflect sadly that I wouldn't be allowing them to get in such a state if Noah was still on the scene. Then, I suddenly have a brain wave. My iPad is in my bag. Stupid, stupid, stupid. I'd forgotten I'd packed it when we first headed up to Scotland (seems like weeks ago now).

Excitedly, I hurry down to the cabin and rummage through my bag. After a couple of anxious minutes, I finally locate it right at the very bottom, and, feeling more buoyant than I have in days, I triumphantly head back to the cockpit. Sitting down, I flash the iPad up to check I've got both battery and signal, and almost punch the air with glee when the answer's yes. Taking a deep breath, I pause and decide a coffee might be in order to keep me going while I surf. I wonder if Ben has any brandy to put in it...

Half an hour later I'm wishing heartily that I could put the clock back and am really tempted to throw the bloody iPad in the river. Sometimes ignorance really is bliss. Firstly, it appears that my father has handed himself in to the Met – there are pictures all over the net of him going into the police station in Belgravia. This all happened yesterday afternoon, so he's obviously been in a holding cell overnight. I know this was his plan all along, but it doesn't stem the irrational fear that I'll never see him again.

And worse - all my efforts to keep Noah out of the hideous mess have been for nothing. The kind, wonderful, amazing, not to mention totally stupid, man has given an interview to the press. A live one. The kind where I can torture myself by watching him talk, hear his sexy voice as he defends both me and my father.

And tells the world we're not together anymore.

'So, Noah, what makes you think Charles Shackleford is innocent of the allegation made against him?'

'I know the guy. He's an honourable man - totally Queen and country and all that; your quintessential British Officer through and through (he obviously doesn't mention any of the quintessential British Officer exploits my father has entertained him with over the months.) He just wouldn't kill someone in cold blood. It goes against everything he believes in.'

'So, you're saying he has your support, Noah?'

'One hundred percent. I'd trust Admiral Shackleford with my life. And I'm saying categorically that he would not, could not, have done this thing.' I gasp. The complete idiot, what the hell is he doing? The all too familiar tears begin to gather in the corner of my eyes.

'And what about your relationship with his daughter, Victory? How's that holding up under the strain? It must be difficult being involved with someone whose father could very possibly be on trial for murder.'

'Victory and I aren't together anymore, but it has nothing to do with what's happened to her father. She's an amazing person who really doesn't deserve all the stupid immature threats she's received.' (What threats? Maybe it really is a good thing I've been out of action.)

'We are still great friends, and she knows she has my support right down the line.'

I pause the video and stare hungrily at the still photo, tears streaming unchecked down my cheeks. Wherever he is, the weather is dull and misty, with rolling green hills in the distance – Ireland. He'd told me that's where he was going next, and Kit had confirmed it. Then I lean back and close my eyes, scrubbing the tears away with the back of my hand. I feel Dotty jump onto my lap and stand on her back legs to lick anxiously at my salty face. Holding her to me, I rest my head against hers, like always, deriving comfort from her furry warmth.

He's put himself on the line for me, done exactly what I asked him not to. Totally risked his career and everything he's worked so hard for. And I've never loved him as much as I do at this moment. What on earth did I do to earn the love and trust from such an amazing, gorgeous man, and how could I have been so stupid as to throw it all away? I let myself go, and sob noisily into Dotty's fur as I recall his parting words to me.

He was right, it *was* all about me. Me and my ridiculous notion that I somehow didn't deserve him. I realize that I'd put him on a pedestal. Refused to accept that he's not some cardboard cutout, there to be swooned over and kept in a corner, but a normal man with normal wants, needs and desires. And he'd chosen me. *Me*, Victory Britannia Shackleford. He loved me and wanted so badly to prove it to me. So, what did I do? I threw it back in his face.

I'm so angry with myself and, irrationally, with him. He could at least have had the decency to let me sacrifice myself on my altar of idiocy so I could continue with my misguided martyrdom, telling everyone who's prepared to listen how I saved Noah Westbrook's career.

Against my will, I picture myself a sad lonely old maid, avidly watching and reading about Noah's exploits, cutting out and saving lurid pictures of him having fun with various Gaynor Andrews lookalikes, all the while telling myself I'd done it for him.

Never has martyrdom looked so unappealing, or so chillingly foolish. For one brief horrible second, I almost hope his act *has* ruined his acting career, so I can tell myself I did the right thing, but the appalling thought disappears as quickly as it came, and I'm simply left with a sort of sad numbness.

It's all much too late for regrets.

By the time Ben drops off Kit about six, I've pretty much got my emotions back under control, although my composure slips a bit as the first thing she says as she climbs on board is, 'Bloody hell, you look awful. What have you got stuck in your hair?' So, I recount my adventures of two nights ago while I uncork the wine and she unwraps our dinner - turning it into a hilariously funny story, which I'm so very good at.

Her laughter makes me feel good, if only for a little while. However, sitting up top, eating fish and chips out of the paper with our fingers (which really is the only way to eat them), she looks at me perceptively and I realize I haven't fooled her at all. She's been my best friend for pretty much ever, and sometimes she knows me better than I know myself. 'You've heard what's happened then?' she says simply. I nod my head, not trusting myself to answer, and for the moment she leaves it at that. I'm absurdly grateful for her sensitivity, and we finish our dinner in relatively comfortable silence while Dotty darts between us doing her usual "poor little me, I'm starving" routine.

At length, after we've eaten and topped up our wine glasses, I realize I can't avoid it any longer. 'I know my dad's in jail Kit,' I say, 'And I've watched Noah playing the hero.' The last is said with a bit more mockery than I intend, and Kit winces and frowns at my tone. As she opens her mouth to answer, I sigh and hold up my hand. 'I know, I'm being a bitch, you don't have to tell me. But Kit, why on earth did he do it?'

'Have you seen the other interview doing the rounds?' she

responds, 'The one with the woman who's accusing your father?' I shake my head in surprise. 'Well, I'm assuming that's why he did it.'

'Is it bad then?' I hurriedly put down the congealing remains of my dinner and go for my iPad, searching for breaking news. The interview isn't hard to find. The woman definitely looks older than my father, and I can't help but speculate that the years can't have been very kind to her. She speaks in rapid Thai, which is interpreted by a voice over, together with subtitles.

The gist? She spotted my father during the worldwide TV coverage of *The Bridegroom* premier in London, and recognised him as the man who, along with a few friends, used her establishment back in the seventies. When questioned about her ability to identify a man after forty years, she switches to broken English, 'He old and ugly now but he in my head always.' Then she swaps back to her native language, saying that she could never forget the face of the man who murdered her husband. When asked why Charles Shackleford had done such a thing, she responds that he and his friends did not want to pay for the services received, trying instead to make a run for it. Apparently, when her husband attempted to stop them, my father turned on him with a knife, coldly and pitilessly stabbing him in the stomach.

I look up at Kit, feeling sick, the fish and chips sitting in my stomach like lumps of lead. 'It's a lie,' I whisper, and she nods reassuringly. 'Everyone who knows the Admiral will recognise that, Tory. Despite his foibles, your father's well-loved in Dartmouth, and there's a lot of support building for him. The town is crawling with reporters, anxious to talk to anyone who knows him, and they're speaking with folks equally keen to put the record straight where the Admiral's character is concerned.

'The problem is not the locals, it's the rest of the world. Individuals who've never met him are calling for his blood, as much to bring you down as him, it has to be said. You know what arseholes people can be when they're jealous. That's why Noah spoke out.'

'And what are they saying about Noah?' I need to know, even if I don't want to. She looks at me intently for a moment, reading me like a book, before answering quietly, 'Not much at the moment, but it's gathering momentum. So far, none of it's negative.'

I look away from her and gaze unseeing over the beautiful landscape around me. My earlier control is vanishing faster than you can say, 'Silly cow,' and I want to scream at the unfairness of it all. In the end, I turn a haunted face back to Kit and say simply, 'Let's get drunk.'

I wake with a start to the sound of my mobile phone ringing. Blinking, I fumble around to find it, before putting it to my ear mumbling, 'Yes?'

'VICTORY, IS THAT YOU?' My father's voice echoes around the little cabin, causing a previously snoring Dotty to struggle her way out of the depths of the duvet, growling.

'Dad?' I respond around the sudden lump in my throat, 'Where are you? Are you okay?'

'Never better,' is his cheerful reply, thankfully, at a level of decibels less likely to render our conversation available to anyone within a half a mile radius. 'It's over, Victory. They released me this morning. I told you it was all a fart in a thunderstorm.' Struggling to keep up, I glance down at my watch to see it's nearly ten am.

'What happened,' I ask, desperate to know whether this is just a temporary development before I finally allow the almost hysterical relief to bubble up from the deep dark pit I'd determinedly shoved it down to when I first heard his voice.

'All the allegations have been dropped,' he answers jovially, as usual, completely oblivious to the terrified concern in my voice. 'Didn't expect it to happen so quickly though, I must admit. Seems like Hugo's son Jason's got a few connections. Anyway, the vultures weren't expecting it either, so I scarpered while they were still scrambling to get into position outside the station.'

As he continues speaking, I finally allow the relief to surface. 'Where are you now?' I ask, hardly able to believe that the nightmare might actually be over.

'On the train. Thought I'd hole up in the Admiralty before anyone else gets wind of it. So give it a couple more days, and then you can get your arse back home. Victory, my girl, we're in the clear.'

I suddenly realise that my father still thinks I'm in Scotland, and for a second, I'm tempted not to enlighten him - let the old bugger worry for a change. Then I relent. Irresponsible and reckless he may be, but I'm positive even he hasn't come through this unscathed, despite the customary good humour in his tone.

'I'm already home, Dad – I mean in Dartmouth, not the Admiralty. We started out pretty soon after you left for London, and I'm currently hiding on board Ben Sheppherd's yacht. It's not exactly a cabin cruiser, but it's moored in the middle of the river, well away from prying eyes.'

There's a slight pause, and his next words prove my supposition correct. 'I'm really glad you're back, Tory,' he says thickly. 'I'll be home soon, and we'll put this cake and arse party behind us.'

'Call me when you're back in the house; we'll talk then,' I respond quietly, cutting the call before he can ask me about Noah.

I stay on the yacht for another two days, then, in the dead of night, I'm sneaked back to the Admiralty in a covert operation that would have done credit to the Special Forces. Freddy is dressed entirely in black leather (any excuse) and insists on referring to me as the package, whenever he has to report our position to Jimmy who's waiting anxiously on shore to help me off Ben's dinghy.

The disembarkation point is apparently a small, neglected pontoon halfway between Kingswear and the Admiralty. There's a path leading up into the woods, and the plan is to slip me into the Admiralty gardens through a newly created, though currently concealed, gap in the fence bordering the sloping woodland.

As I'm helped out of the dinghy and struggle up the hill behind Freddy and Jimmy, I wonder if either of them considered Dotty's penchant for barking loudly at absolutely everything, no matter how trivial, when they were planning their undercover operation. At the moment she seems content to trot along quite happily (and quietly), taking our midnight jaunt in her doggy stride, but as she dashes off up the slope, I glance up at her anxiously - sound carries terribly in these woods. Perhaps I should have let Kit take her off the yacht earlier.

Then I tell myself to get a grip. This is hardly a life-or-death operation, despite Freddy's James Bond costume, and do I really think I'm so important that journalists would actually stay up all night to get an exclusive? Chuckling softly at my ridiculous sense of self-importance, I relax slightly and actually begin to enjoy the walk. I've been cooped up for too long, and it feels so good to finally be able to stride out.

Half an hour later, we're crawling through the gap in the fence, and it's Freddy who makes all the noise - all of a sudden stopping dead and wailing about the damage to his best leather trousers caught on a stray splinter...

Chapter Fifteen

In the end, my fame is relatively short lived. Once the paparazzi accepted that my relationship with Noah Westbrook was over, they quickly lost interest in watching the Admiralty, preferring to do any hanging around outside Noah's house further round the headland. Eventually though, when Noah failed to materialize, they gave up their vigil even there, and life moved on.

Dad has persistently refused to tell me the whole story, saying it isn't entirely his to tell. He did reiterate that the accusations were false and that he'd had information to prove it. It had only taken a meeting with somebody I'd never heard of in the Home Office to sort the *bit of a problem* out - although, it might have taken weeks for Hugo to secure an interview if it hadn't been for his son. Turns out Jason has connections from his Cambridge days (figures – he had to be intelligent as well as gorgeous, even if he is a knob...)

We haven't really spoken about Noah, despite my father's best efforts. He knows the bare bones, but I can't really bring myself to say any more. I just want to try and put it behind me and get on with my life.

Some hope. Four weeks after my homecoming, I find the key to Noah's house in a side pocket of my bag. The pain feels as though I've been punched in the stomach. I've studiously avoided watching the TV or reading the papers, so I have no idea where he is or what he's doing. I do know that my worries about the damage to Noah's career were completely unrealised. If anything, his popularity has soared. Way to go me...

At first, I did entertain a forlorn hope that once my dad was exonerated, he would come to see me, but as the weeks passed and he didn't appear, even that small hope faded, until now I've come to accept that it really is over between us. I'm getting better, but everything just seems so colourless. Even the Regatta, usually so much fun, was just another hurdle to get through, and I'm beginning to wonder whether it might be better for me to move away, to somewhere I'm not reminded of the life I stupidly threw away every time I cross the river and look up towards the headland.

The weather for mid-September was unusually warm. Although the trees were beginning to shed their leaves as autumn approached, and the nights were beginning to get chilly, the days continued sunny and hot.

The Admiral was sitting outside the Ship with Pickles, waiting for Jimmy. While things had gone back pretty much to the way they were before Hollywood had intruded, the Admiral was wise enough to understand that something had nevertheless fundamentally altered between him and Jimmy.

Although he wouldn't have recognised it as such, the difference could be attributed to respect. Jimmy was no longer a subordinate, subject to the Admiral's whims – well at least not at the weekend anyway. They were on a much more equal footing, and strangely enough, Charles Shackleford was content with that – mostly...

Now though, as he waited impatiently for Jimmy to arrive, he was determined to enlist his friend's help. He couldn't possibly sit and watch Victory's miserable face for one minute longer. Although his daughter had given her blessing to him and Mabel getting hitched, the Admiral conceded that two women in a kitchen was one too many. He knew Victory intended to move out once the nuptials were over, but he felt like he'd come full circle. It was left to him as usual to sort the whole bloody mess out. Of course, he'd have to track the bloke down first.

In the end, it was another ten minutes before Jimmy arrived, and to the Admiral's amazed disbelief, he actually had his wife in tow. This was so incredible that for a moment, words failed him as he thought he was seeing a mirage. Pickles, the traitor, ambled happily up to the harpy, and, completely oblivious to his master's sense of what was right and proper, held up his head for a fuss.

'What would you like to drink, dear?' Jimmy's request was nervous, even to the Admiral's insensitive ears, so at least he was aware of the enormity of this breach of protocol. Charles Shackleford jumped up, unwilling to be abandoned for even a minute with the woman he'd only exchanged half a dozen words with in nearly forty years.

Horrifyingly, however, Emily put her hand on his arm, saying, 'Charlie, stay where you are. Jim will get me a drink.' Completely lost for words, the Admiral sat back down and watched longingly as his friend disappeared into the dim interior of the pub. Taking a sip of his pint, he looked anywhere except at the woman seated next to him.

'Don't worry, Charlie, I won't be staying long. I just wanted to have a quiet word with you.' Against his will, the Admiral felt a slight quickening of interest, which he did his best to hide, glancing over at Emily with a frown. 'I know you want Jim to help you sort out your daughter's love life,' she said flatly, 'And we all know just how successful that was the last time you meddled.' The Admiral opened his mouth to protest, but the bloody woman unbelievably held up her hand to indicate that she hadn't finished. What a bollocking cheek. Still, it did the trick, and he subsided reluctantly, while looking longingly to see if Jimmy was on his way back. No such luck, so he sighed and waved the harpy to continue what he assumed was about to be a blistering lecture.

Which is why her next words caught him completely by surprise. 'I want to help. If you're to stand any chance of getting this stupid mess sorted out between Tory and her actor, you're going to need a woman's input.' She glanced over to the slowly opening door where Jimmy was struggling with the drinks. 'Well don't just stand there, go and give him a bloody hand.' To his internal amazement Charles Shackleford found himself climbing out of his chair to hold open the door. He felt like crying.

Jimmy placed the drinks down on the table, and the Admiral was relieved to see that one was for him. He had a feeling he was going to need it. 'A bag of pork scratchings for you, my dove,' was all Jimmy said, handing the small packet to his wife with a flourish as though he'd just offered her keys to a Porsche. She simpered back. Bloody simpered. And in response, Jimmy smiled and kissed her on the cheek. The Admiral was quite simply appalled. Was this the sort of treatment Mabel was expecting?

He took a large draught of his pint in an effort to repress a sudden sinking feeling. However, before he could plunge further into the deep dark hole that was suddenly the prospect of matrimony, Emily patted Jimmy's knee and spoke again, dropping a complete bombshell with all the aplomb of someone who knows she has her listener by the short and curlies. 'I have it on good authority that Noah Westbrook will be back in Dartmouth sometime over the next forty-eight hours.' She looked at both men, self-satisfaction evident in her expression, clearly saying, 'If you want something done right, get a woman to do it.'

All thoughts of matrimony, painless or otherwise, were completely forgotten as the Admiral turned towards Emily, impatiently waiting for her to elaborate. As she started to smile smugly, obviously relishing the situation, the Admiral was finally forced to give her the stare - the one known to drive subordinates to gibbering idiots in five seconds flat. It didn't quite have that effect on Jimmy's wife, but her smugness definitely slipped a bit, and she was gratifyingly quick to continue. 'Gladys Taylor got a call from her agency instructing her to go up to a certain house to give it a good clean and open it up ready for the owner. Course Gladys doesn't know whose house it is...'

Charles Shackleford leaned back in his chair and nodded his head slowly. He wasn't surprised to hear Emily's news. This was just another sign from up top that he was destined to fix the disaster that was his daughter's love life. Again. He gave a self-righteous sigh and took another swallow of his beer, quickly dismissing the source of his information as his mind feverishly began working on a plan.

However, Emily Noon did not intend to be cast aside quite so easily, and leaning forward, she fixed the Admiral with a look of her own that had been known to cause grown men to run for the hills. 'So, exactly when are you going to tell Tory?'

Dotty and I are strolling along one of the many pathways that meander through the woods up the side of the valley behind the Admiralty. Well, I'm strolling – Dotty as always is dashing about, searching for that ultimate treasure - the foulest smell possible to take back to Pickles as a present. I keep a close eye on her as we make our way through the trees.

Although the early afternoon is warm and sunny, evidence of the coming autumn is everywhere, from the russets and golds of the trees to the satisfying crunch of the leaves fallen to the ground early. Spying a few wild blackberry bushes, I fish around in my pocket for a bag and spend an enjoyable half an hour picking the ripe berries, alternating them between the bag and my mouth. Dotty, whose list of edible treats does not apparently include blackberries, takes the opportunity to have a well-earned nap, sunning herself in a small patch of sunlight that's managed to penetrate the dense canopy.

The mundane task helps to take my mind off my ongoing internal war. I really am driving myself up the wall, not to mention Kit and Freddy who have, bless them, endless patience, and my father who unfortunately does not. His latest observation, offered earlier today as he slammed out of the house, was that my face was beginning to resemble that of a bulldog who's just licked piss off a nettle, and I should bollocking well stop mooning around and make an effort to "grow a pair."

And, while others might have put it a little more sympathetically, I know he's right. Despite the temptation to lay all my current problems at my father's insensitive door, I realize, deep in my heart, that I've only got myself to blame for my current situation.

I've studiously avoided going over to the other side of the river since getting completely, blindly trollied during Regatta week and performing a drunken rendition of *What'll I Do Without You* while taking sobbing gulps of my gin and tonic in between verses. Unfortunately caught on camera, the resulting video was standing at nearly two million hits on YouTube as of this morning. But one drunken karaoke going viral is unlikely to cause the end of the world as we know it (although I've so far resisted reading the comments), and I can't continue to eschew all human contact forever – not least because I need to start earning a living again now I'm no longer Noah Westbrook's personal interior designer (oh God, please don't let him have seen the video).

So, before setting out on my walk, I called Kit to ask if she fancied a drink at the Cherub after closing up the gallery later on today. Her enthusiasm ratcheted up the guilt a couple of notches, especially as her life is not exactly going according to plan at the moment.

After therapeutically clearing the bushes of every berry within reaching distance, I wipe my juice-stained hands on my jeans, and glance down at my watch, surprised to note it's nearly three thirty. I'm supposed to be meeting Kit just after five, so I hurriedly tie off my bag and, waking Dotty from her impromptu siesta, we head quickly down the trail towards the Admiralty. I haven't a clue what I'm going to do with all the blackberries I've picked – there are only so many apple and blackberry pies I can fit in the freezer, and jam making is definitely not one of my many talents. As I plonk my prize on the kitchen table fifteen minutes later, I wonder whether I should just give them to Mabel. She looks like she might be a bit of a jam making groupie. Decision made, I write a short note for Dad and slip it under the bag before heading upstairs for a quick shower, Dotty trotting enthusiastically at my heels. She knows we're heading up to her second favourite place in the whole wide world after the kitchen – my bed. And, after all that exercise, she's more than ready for another snooze.

As the ferry bumps up the slipway on the other side just over an hour later, I can't help but notice the Floating Bridge next to the slip is heaving, every table filled with tourists making the most of the early evening sun before it becomes too cold to sit outside. Glad of my sunglasses, I quickly make my way off the ferry and away from any prying eyes. Sadly, my spontaneous and unique karaoke performance whilst under the influence has most definitely rekindled the public's interest in my activities, with everyone and his dog waiting in breathless anticipation to see what I'll do next to make a complete tit of myself. Today however, I am determined to stay well and truly, not to mention boringly, sober, so my less than adoring voyeuristic fans can go screw themselves...

Kit is already seated in the corner when Dotty and I arrive, and there's an open bottle of wine ready and waiting on the table. 'Boringly sober,' I remind myself as I sit down opposite and watch her pour me a glass. My faithless furry companion has already abandoned me in favour of my best friend who, in addition to the wine, is also in possession of an opened packet of crisps – a fact that Dotty no doubt clocked within nanoseconds of entering the pub. 'To starting over,' I murmur as we clink glasses. To my dismay, Kit's response to my toast is more like a grimace than a smile, and I can't help but watch, concerned as she knocks back half her glass of wine in one gulp. 'Are your mum and Dad still coming over at the end of the month?' I ask quietly.

'I think so,' is her miserable reply. 'I've told them I've got too much stock for them to put the gallery on the market immediately. They have to give me time to at least recoup some of the losses.'

I shake my head in disbelief, unable to get my head around what's happened. 'What did they say?'

'They're prepared to give me until the end of October. Apparently, they've already got a potential buyer. Someone they met in France. He wants to pay cash.'

'What are you going to do?' I ask, not knowing what else to say, helplessly watching her take another long gulp of wine before refilling her glass.

'Find a job before I'm homeless,' she answers flatly at length.

'You'll never be homeless, Kitty Kat,' I respond gently. 'You know there's always a place for you at the Admiralty.' To my horror, she suppresses a sudden sob, and I reach out my hand, saying lightly, 'Just think, the two of us can wreak havoc in Mabel's kitchen.' She grasps my outstretched hand and laughs tearfully. 'It will all work out, Kit. You'll see,' I continue, my words of reassurance as much for myself as for my best friend. 'What did my mum use to say? - When one door closes, another one always opens.'

'The darkest hour is just before dawn,' she offers ruefully. We clink our glasses again, this time in calm acknowledgement that the bad times will pass.

'O.M.G, I've arrived just in time. One more minute and you'd have gone all Thelma and Louise on me, and the next thing I know I'm talking you out of driving yourselves over a cliff...'

'Did you invite him?' I ask Kit over Dotty's ecstatic welcoming bark.

'I might have happened to mention I was seeing you tonight,' is her doleful response. 'Although I could have sworn I said I wasn't totally sure but thought we were meeting in the Dartmouth Arms.'

'You don't think I can spot a porky pie coming from you a mile off, oh queen of prevaricators? Puleease, how long have I known you?' Freddy's answer is dismissive as he seats himself between us, and I can't help but smile. Kit is not quite so tolerant.

'Did you not think, ah, perhaps they haven't told me because they want a girly get-together? Or are you slightly less intuitive than you are nosy?' she asks, eyebrows raised in question.

'I haven't got an intuitive bone in my body, as you well know,' Freddy responds cheerfully, waving at the barman to bring him his usual. 'Now, potential gossip on the other hand...' He rubs his hands gleefully. 'So darlings, what have I missed? Made any more videos lately?' The last is obviously directed at me, and I resist the urge to pour his newly acquired drink over his head.

In the end, we both give in somewhat gracelessly and pour all the misery and angst out to our thick-skinned third. Once done, we stare at him expectantly, waiting for some kind of astounding insight into what is undoubtedly a difficult situation. However, sometimes we have to remember that for all he prides himself in being in touch with his feminine side, at the end of the day, Freddy is still a man. And his response to Kit's outpouring of despair just goes to prove it.

'If you have to give up your flat, can I have first refusal?'

Chapter Sixteen

The Admiral managed to get through two whole days before he decided to take matters into his own hands. He told himself that he wasn't going to actually do anything, just have a quick shufti, spy out the lay of the land, so to speak. After all, he couldn't be sure whether Noah was truly back in Dartmouth. Once he'd done a quick recce, he could then assess the situation and go to Victory with a full report. Capital plan.

He arranged to meet Jimmy in the Ship at half past seven, ostensibly for a quick drink. His sneaky strategy was to divulge the mission details to his reluctant accomplice once they'd had a pint. That way, the dragon wasn't likely to get wind of anything beforehand, and Jimmy was less likely to chicken out.

He'd thought briefly about conducting this operation by himself but had quickly abandoned the idea. As much as it galled him to admit it, Jimmy's prudence and caution had proved invaluable on more than one occasion. He might joke that Jimmy was usually ignored so much his name should be Terms and Conditions, but in light of their newly discovered equality, the Admiral deemed that if there was even the remotest chance he was going to end up in the shit, then it was only fair that Jimmy should do so too.

At twenty-five to eight, the Admiral pushed open the door to the Ship. Normally, exactly on time, it had taken him longer than anticipated to put his combat gear on. The last time he'd worn it was to a fancy dress do at the Kingswear village hall ten years ago. There was an outside possibility that he'd put a smidgeon of weight on since then.

To the Admiral's satisfaction, Jimmy was already sitting on his stool next to the bar, however the look of alarm that quickly spread across his face when he spied his former commanding officer had the Admiral reflecting that being a few minutes adrift might actually have worked in his favour - mainly due to the fact he was completely blocking the door should Jimmy try to make a run for it.

Watching the Admiral approach the bar dressed like a Geriatric Mutant Ninja Turtle caused every alarm bell in Jimmy's head to ring loudly and repeatedly. Nevertheless, he didn't move, totally rooted to the spot like the rest of the Ship's Thursday night regulars. Fortunately, Charles Shackleford was totally oblivious to the impact his chosen attire was having on the occupants of the pub, being entirely focused on the pint ready and waiting for him on the bar. There was a sudden loud, though very brief, ripping sound which caused the Admiral to pause for a second in the act of hoisting himself up onto the bar stool, but when nothing more ominous followed, he sat himself down with a grunt and, sighing happily, took a sip of his beer.

The two men sat in silence for a few moments while the Admiral took the time to savour his pint, and Jimmy frantically tried to come up with a valid reason to leave. However, unable to concoct a convincing excuse in the necessary time frame, the small man finally exhaled noisily, picked up his own pint and simply resigned himself to waiting.

An hour later, Jimmy found himself driving slowly and carefully up the narrow road winding around the headland towards Noah's house, all the while wondering how the hell he'd managed to get himself embroiled in another of the Admiral's bloody harebrained schemes, and exactly what he was going to tell Emily when she found out about it. His heart was sinking faster than you could say 'Cowabunga,' and his only teeny weensy consolation was the Admiral's nonchalant claim that he wasn't intending to actually speak to Noah if the actor happened to be at the house - just spy on him. Jimmy's sarcastic, 'Oh, well of course, that makes it all fine then,' fell on completely deaf ears.

He moaned softly. This could end in a divorce. Emily had been so adamant that the information about Noah's return be turned over to Tory for her to decide whether she wanted to do anything about it. The only reason she hadn't done it herself was due to Jimmy's belief that such sensitive information should come from her father. What the bollocking hell was he thinking? The Admiral was about as sensitive as a frostbitten big toe.

As Jimmy carefully negotiated the twists and turns in the gathering dusk, his lurid imagination already had him reduced to living in a bedsit with only lice and cockroaches for company after Emily had callously taken him to the cleaners. He got as far as wondering whether he should stock up on cardboard boxes when suddenly the callous, cold-hearted perpetrator of all his suffering tapped him on the shoulder. 'Stop here, Jimmy lad and park the car next to that bush.'

Carefully manoeuvring the car so that it faced back the way they'd come (obviously in case they needed a quick getaway), Jimmy finally turned off the engine. They were parked underneath a low canopy of trees, practically on top of the bush the Admiral had earmarked, and now the light was almost gone, only someone deliberately scouting the vicinity would likely notice their car. It would have to do, especially as Jimmy had flatly refused to climb one of the trees to cut down a few branches when the Admiral suggested they needed a bit more camouflage. Of course, the trees hanging over a hundred foot drop directly into the river might have had something to do with Jimmy's reluctance, although the Admiral privately thought his friend was being a bit of a nancy.

Looking behind him, Jimmy spotted Noah's house about thirty yards away. From this angle, he couldn't see any lights. 'Shall I stay in the car?' he suggested hopefully. 'You know, in case we need to scarper quickly.' For a second, he thought he was in luck as the Admiral frowned and pursed his lips, obviously weighing up the pros and cons. To Jimmy's dismay, however, the Admiral finally shook his head reluctantly.

'Good plan, Jimmy boy but wouldn't want you to miss out on all the fun,' was his perfectly serious comment, completely missing Jimmy's look of incredulity in the dark. 'Anyway, we're a team and it'll need both of us, a seamless unit working together as one entity to get even one of us over that bloody fence…'

Five minutes later, they were standing next to the six-foot fence in question. 'I know for a fact he hasn't got any alarms on this bugger yet,' the Admiral confided in a stage whisper that could have been heard twenty yards away. 'You stand on my shoulders and have a look to see if there are any lights on.' He bent down and cupped his hands together, a clear indication that Jimmy should place a foot in the cradle created and simply hop onto the larger man's shoulders.

Taking a deep breath, Jimmy obediently lifted his left foot and placed a hand on each shoulder. Then doing a small hopping motion that nearly resulted in his left knee shoving the Admiral's chin up his nostrils, he levered himself up. Once there, it became quickly apparent that this was as far as he was going. He briefly tried to lift his right leg, currently swinging freely, over the Admiral's shoulder, but, although it might have been different thirty years ago, the necessary twisting motion to complete the action was completely beyond him, and he was much more likely to take out the Admiral's eye.

For a few seconds, they stood there swaying gently, Jimmy's scrotum unfortunately pressed against the Admiral's face as though they were taking part in a bizarre porn movie. 'Can you see anything?' The muffled voice coming from his nether regions jolted Jimmy out of his paralysis, and, precariously transferring his hold onto the Admiral's head, the small man carefully looked over the fence. At first, he thought the house was empty, but after his human scaffold wobbled to the right a bit, he could see lights shining onto the lawn around the side of the house.

'I think there's someone inside,' he hissed down, just as the hall lights came on.

∞∞∞∞

We resist the temptation to get drunk, instead taking solace in carbohydrates – a decision Dotty roundly applauds. By the end of the first bowl of chips, we manage to come up with a list of employment possibilities that are likely to pay more than minimum wage and thus avoid the likelihood of Kit having to move into her garage.

Despite his initial unthinking remark, Freddy turns out to be very adroit at thinking outside the box, and by the time I finally tear Dotty away from the remains of our third bowl of chips to catch the last ferry, Kit is looking much less haunted. As I leave, I bend down and pull her into a quick tight hug. 'Please try not to worry too much, Kitty Kat. We'll sort it out together.'

Half an hour later, as Dotty and I are walking up the steep slope that is the Admiralty garden, I'm still mulling over our inventory of opportunities and suddenly realise that for once, I'm not wallowing in self-pity. This is pretty much the first time I've thought of anything but my own misery since Noah and I split up. While I hate to see my best friend in so much turmoil, I can't deny that it's a relief to think about something other than my own stupidity - it has to be said, self-flagellation gets old very quickly.

My sense of satisfaction is relatively short lived however, as by the time I finally arrive breathless and gasping at the back door, my ability to construct any kind of coherent thought has practically disappeared. I do this trek nearly every day. I just can't understand why I'm not stick thin. I pause at the door, intending to take a quick breather before rummaging around for my house key which for a reason only understood by handbag fairies, always seems to migrate to the very bottom of whatever holdall I'm carrying, usually necessitating the ritual tipping out of everything, from tampons to dog treats, to find it.

I'm just about to drag the bag over my head when suddenly, the door is yanked open from inside the kitchen, causing me to stumble back in surprise. 'Bloody hell, Dad, you scared the crap out of me. What on earth are you doing sitting in the dark?' I step past him to turn on the kitchen light. 'Why on earth are you dressed like you're an extra out of *The Dirty Doz...*' I stammer to a halt as I look up at my father's solemn face. 'Think you'd better sit down, Victory,' he murmurs in a voice so far below his usual level of decibels it causes my heart to jolt in sick response. 'I've got something to tell you.'

Suddenly, faced with an almost uncontainable desire to be anywhere but here, Jimmy nevertheless resisted the urge to turn into Captain America and use the Admiral's head as a trampoline to vault over the fence into the still dark garden beyond. Instead, both men froze, each frantically trying to come up with a credible reason as to why they were imitating a Native American totem pole outside Noah Westbrook's front door. After a few seconds however, the Admiral began to wobble alarmingly. While not particularly heavy, Jimmy's death like grip on the Admiral's balding head, not to mention the fact that he was slowly but surely being suffocated by his close proximity to his friend's one-eyed trouser snake, meant that things were going downhill quicker than you could say, 'Have-um heap big problem.'

As the Admiral began to totter blindly towards the fence, Jimmy made a grab for the nearest wooden post. Muttering to the larger man to stand still, he eventually managed to swing his free leg over the wooden railing, finally lifting his weight from the Admiral's shoulders but leaving him balancing precariously on the top of the fence. Both men glanced anxiously towards the front door, behind which they could now clearly hear voices. 'Hide,' whispered the Admiral urgently, giving Jimmy a sharp push before taking off at a staggering hobble towards the trees hiding their car. Fortunately, the only sound Jimmy made as he toppled sideways was a barely audible woomph, just as the door opened to reveal Noah Westbrook.

Tucking himself into the shadows, Charles Shackleford watched as Noah stepped outside. 'Can you see anything, hon?' came a voice from inside.

A woman's voice.

The Admiral felt like someone had punched him in the stomach. He was rooted to the spot as he watched the owner of the voice come up behind Noah to lean her cheek against his and wrap her arms around his neck. Noah raised his hand to lightly, familiarly, touch the fingers pressed against his chest. 'Nothing,' he murmured, 'Must have been the wind. I'll get the alarms checked while we're here.' The woman nodded, giving him a quick peck on the cheek before dropping her arms and retracing her steps back into the house. After staring intently into the near darkness for a few more seconds, Noah turned back to join her, closing the door decisively behind him.

A minute or so later the hall lights went out and silence reigned, apart from Jimmy's muffled swearing as he blundered about behind the fence. The Admiral knew he should be grateful that his friend had survived the fall unscathed, but all he could see was his daughter's heartbroken face when he told her that Noah Westbrook had another woman.

∞∞∞

Dad insists on sitting me down at the kitchen table, which already has a large glass of wine placed on it ready and waiting. For me. Before I can speak however, he bangs out of the kitchen to fetch a bottle of port from his study. With a sense of grim foreboding, I watch him pour himself a large measure - I can see he's working out in his head exactly how to tell me something awful. As I take a large sip of my wine, I want to shout at him to just spit out whatever he has to say, but I know from old that such a strategy doesn't work with my father. He'll speak in his own time or not at all. My heart lurches sickeningly between possibilities, the chief of which is that it's all been a big mistake, and he's actually going to jail after all...

By the time he finally seats himself down opposite me at the kitchen table, I'm ready to scream. My glass is already half empty which my father ominously acknowledges with a satisfied nod. 'The thing is, Victory,' he starts, just as I'm about to tip the rest of the wine over his head, 'What I mean to say is... Oh bollocks girl, there's no good way to say this. The fact is, Noah's gone and got himself another woman.'

It was the last thing I expected him to say. I stare at him in silence, my head trying to process what my heart is completely repudiating. 'How do you know?' I whisper finally.

'Saw him,' is Dad's blunt response. 'He's back in Dartmouth and staying at his pad with her.'

A kaleidoscope of disbelief, misery, loneliness and despair hurtles through my mind. 'Noah's in Ireland, so you must have been mistaken,' I finally manage to croak, the pain almost choking me. My father sighs and shakes his head. 'I wasn't mistaken, Victory love. Jimmy and I went up to his house earlier. He was there.'

'But – but did he see you? Did you speak to him?' My voice is thick with unshed tears.

'No, he didn't know we were there,' Dad replies brusquely, 'But I saw him at the door with this stunner. She put her arms around him and kissed him.' I know my father isn't being deliberately cruel. He calls a spade a spade, and bugger wrapping it up in social niceties. I feel myself curl up into a tight ball of mental anguish. How - how could he *do* this? How could he take someone else there so *soon*? Oh God, I think I'm going to be sick. I shove my chair back so hard in my haste to stand, that it falls to the floor with a crash. Without stopping to right it, I rush out of the kitchen and up the stairs to my bedroom. I only just manage to make it to the bathroom before the chips I so enjoyed earlier decide to make another appearance. Then, after retching into the toilet bowl until nothing is left, I finally collapse on to the bathroom floor, and wedged between the toilet and the radiator, I bury my head in my hands and cry.

It's three o'clock in the morning, and I'm still wide awake. The tears have finally dried up. My mind has been replaying our breakup in minute-by-minute high definition, over and over again since I got into bed, and now, all I can hear in my head behind the incessant pounding is Noah, saying, 'You *know* me, Tory.'

And I do.

I've touched him, kissed him, teased him and made love with him. He's not a god. He's flesh and blood. Sincere and genuine. He doesn't need others to fawn over him and remind him of his self-worth. I'm well aware that I'm no Charlize Theron. No amount of effort is going to transform me from plain, plump, ordinary

Victory Shackleford to a glamour goddess. But I was enough for him. More than enough.

He was mine...

But I couldn't believe it because I wouldn't *let* myself believe it. The only obstacle in the way of my relationship with Noah was me.

And it still is.

I sit up in bed suddenly, causing Dotty to grumble softly. Frowning into the gloom, I take a deep breath. Who do I want to be? Do I want to be *this?* Insecure and so obsessed with other people's ideas about who I am that I throw away the love of my life because I don't think I fit the mould of a movie star's girlfriend?

A sudden fragile hope bursts inside of me. Noah has never seen me as anything but *me.* And I am enough. *As I am.*

But he won't come back to me, even though all the melodrama is over, simply because he knows that the real reason we broke up had nothing to do with my father and everything to do with me. I recall his parting words to me in Bloodstone Tower again. He was right. What we had together wasn't a fairy tale, it was real.

I just have to let go of my own self as an obstacle.

It's funny how sometimes the clearest moments come when you least expect them. My heart thuds in tremulous excitement. I need to tell Noah that finally, I understand what he was trying to say. That I don't care what people say about me, about us.

But, how on earth am I going to do it, and where? I can ask Noah to come to see me, but what if he refuses? If that happens, have I got the balls, as my father would say, to go to him?

Chapter Seventeen

It's just after ten am when I finally wake up to Dotty's insistent pawing. I've spent the better part of the night devising then discarding plan after plan to get Noah's attention - all of which seem incredibly lame, not to mention ridiculous, in the bright light of day, especially when you consider the fact that Noah obviously has someone else. As I wearily climb out of bed and throw on my dressing gown, I'm finally forced to confront the elephant in the room that I'd so determinedly ignored during my late-night deliberations.

I've not got over Noah, but the evidence suggests that he may well have got over me...

As I go downstairs to let Dotty out, there's no sign of my father or Pickles. I'm not surprised. He doesn't do female hysterics very well at all, and it's not like we haven't been here before.

Putting the kettle on, I feel my resolve, so strong in the early hours, begin to fade as harsh reality arrives with the daylight. Am I a fool to think there might be a chance? Am I prepared to humiliate myself on the off chance that Noah might still have feelings for me? What if there are other people there when I see him?

Against my will, I envision Noah's very public rejection, and by the time the kettle has boiled, my head has already had my humiliation being covertly filmed and posted up on You Tube.

Bet that would get more than two million hits.

Dotty's scratching at the door brings me back to the present, and I shudder at the thought of being the laughingstock of pretty much the whole world.

But then there's no sense in doing things in half measures…

Letting Dotty in, I sit down at the table nursing my tea. It's Saturday, so I've got two more days before I have to start making an effort to drum up business. I toy with the idea of phoning Kit, but eventually decide against it. She doesn't need any more of my troubles heaped onto her already overflowing plate. I wonder if I should start writing down a list of possible strategies – it seemed to work with Kit's problems. Yep, feels like a good plan…

Half an hour later I'm sitting chewing my pen, a piece of paper in front of me on which I've written the number one in the top left corner. The rest of the page is covered in heart shaped doodles. Tactics have obviously never been my strong point. Now if this was my father, we'd probably have an operation worthy of inclusion in the top fifty most daring military tactics of all time. Sighing, I put down my pen - as much as my head balks at the whole idea, I think I'm going to have to ask for his help. Suddenly, as if by magic, Pickles dashes through the back door, heralding the great man's arrival, so I get up to put the kettle back on and dig out some biscuits. This could take a while.

I'm just pouring the hot water into the tea pot as Dad finally stomps into the room – at least five minutes behind the elderly Springer. 'That bloody hound'll be the death of me,' he grumbles, leaning on to the kitchen table to get his breath back. 'Can't keep chasing him all over the bloody countryside.'

'You've never chased him anywhere,' I respond mildly over my shoulder. 'Pickles knows these woods like the back of his paws – you couldn't find him because you obviously left the gate open again.'

Responding to my comment with a single grunt, my father looks suspiciously at the tea and biscuits on the table. 'What's this in aid of?' he asks abruptly, and I know he's afraid he's in for another extended blubbering session. It's not that he doesn't care, but Dad's always been a man of action – which is basically the reason he's got himself up the creek without a paddle so many times in the past. He really doesn't do wailing and weeping and ritual hammering of breasts. But that's okay, I'm done wailing and weeping, and I'm ready for action – even if, in truth, I'd prefer to be tied to a chair and forced to listen to Barry Manilow tunes while having my tonsils removed with a rusty spoon...

'I need your help, Dad,' I say, sitting down and shoving the plate of biscuits towards him. He raises his eyebrows slightly and, after a slight pause, sits down – I'm unsure whether that's because of the chocolate digestives in front of him or the fact that he can't pass up a possible opportunity to meddle.

'I need to talk to Noah,' I continue in a rush, wanting to get everything out before he has a chance to speak. 'I can't leave it like this, Dad. I just can't. Our breakup was totally my fault. Noah wanted to support me, he wanted to help, but you know me, I wouldn't let him. There's a real possibility that he hates me now, but I just can't get on with my life without at least trying to put things right.' I take a deep breath, feeling the tears threatening again. 'I still love him, Dad,' I whisper finally, forcing the words through my clogged throat. 'And I need your help to get him back.'

In the end, we go through two packets of chocolate biscuits before we finally come up with the following strategy...

1. Go up to Noah's house.
2. Speak to him.

Seriously, that's my father's cunning plan. After going all round the houses, this is what it boils down to. A plan I could have worked out all by myself. 'There's no bollocking way round it,' is his terse response, when I express my disappointment that his proposed course of action seems to be a trifle less, well, *multifaceted* than his usual schemes. 'He won't come to you, Victory. You know it. I know it. Now, what we don't know is how long he's here. The longer you leave it, the more likely you'll lose him forever to the looker he's currently shacking up with.' I wince visibly, but he continues mercilessly. 'You're not going to bump into him somewhere in Dartmouth. The bloke's not going to risk any chance of running into you accidently. It's either put your money where your mouth is, or leave the poor bugger alone.'

'That's hardly an accurate way to describe Noah Westbrook,' I retort, stung a little by his brutal assessment of the situation.

'You're my daughter, Victory, and I love you, but after listening to your whingeing, I'm beginning to think that any bloke who gets involved with you and your bloody hang-ups is not only a poor bugger, but possibly wants his head testing,' is my father's decisive reply as he gets out of his chair. 'If you want this man, Victory, you've got to step out of your bloody comfort zone and go get him.'

And with that, he stomps off towards his study, yelling to Pickles that if he wanders off again today, he's off to the knackers' yard. I'm assuming he's referring to the dog, not himself...

It's now five o'clock in the afternoon, and I've been pacing up and down my bedroom for the last three hours. Dotty, in the beginning watching me walk back and forth anxiously, got bored about an hour ago and is now snoring happily underneath the covers of my bed. My stomach is in complete knots, and my mind is simply going round in circles.

It's Saturday. What are the odds that Noah's not doing

something potentially romantic with his new love interest on a Saturday night? How can I just turn up in between the Champagne and the chocolate-covered strawberries to announce that I've made a mistake and want him back? But what if he leaves Dartmouth tomorrow morning, and I miss my chance altogether? The thought of that happening when he's so close brings me out in a cold sweat. I glance at the clock for the umpteenth time before sitting down abruptly on the bed, only narrowly missing Dotty's tail. I have to do this. Even if he doesn't want me and tells me so in the most demeaning and public way possible. I. Have. To. Do. This.

Or I'll never forgive myself.

Before I can change my mind, I throw open my wardrobe doors to find a little number that will shout, 'Look what you're missing,' to Noah, when he opens his front door to find his ex standing there, (and which will also make him pause before slamming said door in my face). Helplessly, I stand staring at the row of dresses in front of me. Although my closet is much fuller now than it was before Noah and I became an item, it doesn't mean I'm any better at choosing the right costume for the right occasion. I so wish Kit was here now to help. She'd instinctively know which one to go for.

Hurriedly, I go through the wardrobe, throwing dress after dress on the bed, until Dotty's forced to come up for air or risk being buried alive. Then unexpectedly, I have a sudden epiphany. I know exactly which dress to wear – the navy and white Sophie Loren number I wore the first time Noah and I set eyes on each other. *Perfect.*

It takes me a couple of precious minutes to unearth the dress, and when I finally manage to drag it out, there are more than a few creases, but I'm sure they'll drop out. After giving the armpits an experimental sniff and checking for any stains, I give the dress a hard shake, and we're good to go. Then I add it to the pile on the bed before heading to the bathroom for a quick shower.

Half an hour later, I'm ready. As I stare at myself in the mirror, I realize I've had a song in my head since first getting into the shower. Experimentally, I sing it out loud...

Presto presto
Do your very besto
Don't hang back like a shy little kid
You'll be so glad that you did what you did
If you do it with a Bing Bang Bong
A Bing Bang Bong

Smiling for the first time since my dad dropped his bombshell, I realize the song is from the movie *Houseboat* which Sophia Loren starred in with Cary Grant. I can't believe how appropriate it is. 'Wish me luck, Sophia,' I whisper to the image before marching to the door determinedly, Dotty scurrying behind. Once at the door, I stop so abruptly that the little dog bumps into my heels. In my haste to prepare myself for my potential metaphorical public flogging, I've forgotten a couple of somethings.

How am I going to get there, and who's going to look after Dotty?

Bugger. I can't walk – it would take too long, and besides in these shoes, I'll end up looking more like Quasimodo than Sophia Loren by the time I get there. Of course, I could drive, but two glasses of wine masquerading as Dutch courage have put paid to that. A taxi would just prompt more gossip. Maybe Dad will give me a lift. I can't help but quail at the thought of him being anywhere near Noah's house at the same time as me, but beggars can't be choosers. Hurriedly, I run downstairs, hoping that Dad hasn't gone off to the Ship. Luckily (or not as the case may be), my father's still in his study when I knock.

As he throws open the door, I'm fooled for a second into thinking his expression softens a little on seeing me all dressed up like a dog's dinner, but it's probably a trick of the light. After staring at me for a moment, he says simply, 'So you're going to do the business then?' I nod my head, then suddenly needing some kind of validation, even if it's from someone whose fashion sense is mostly based on what doesn't itch, I ask if I look okay.

To my amazement, he nods his head in approval before saying gruffly, 'You look just like your mother.' Tears fill my eyes in response to his words, and I quickly rummage around in my handbag for a tissue, only to be handed a large square linen handkerchief, pulled from the depths of one of my father's pockets. The gesture takes me back to when I was a child. Dad always had a hankie – wherever we went. It was used to mop up ice cream, bandage knees, blow noses, dry tears – very often all on the same day with the same hankie. The one my father offers me is none too clean either, but I take it, feeling like I'm eight again – warm, secure and, above all, loved. He might not say it often, but I know my father loves me still.

After blowing my nose, I hand the square of linen back to him, and he stuffs it back in his pocket without looking, causing me to wince slightly as I picture its grubby folds. It didn't seem to matter when I was little. 'I don't know how I'm going to get there, Dad,' I murmur, still more than a little immersed in primary school mode. His answer, however, not only snatches off my rose-tinted glasses, but throws them on the floor and tramples on them for good measure.

'Mabel's son Oscar is picking me up in fifteen minutes. I'm going over to her place for dinner. I'm sure he won't mind giving you a lift.'

'You're having dinner with Mabel's son?' I query a little more sharply than I'd intended, suddenly unable to prevent an onslaught of impending stepsibling jealousy to rival Baby Jane at her worst. 'Well, of course Mabel will be there too, and her daughter Amanda,' my father answers, completely oblivious to the green mist now rapidly turning me into Regan from *The Exorcist*.

'Why wasn't I invited?' The aggressively petulant tone of my voice finally gets his attention, and he frowns at me for a second before answering. 'She only asked me this morning after we had our chat. Of course, you were invited, but I told Mabel you had other plans. I was hoping you'd see sense and want to take yourself off to sort things out with the Yank.' He shrugs, indicating his bafflement at the idiosyncrasies of women. 'So, do you want a lift or not?'

His words shove me off my huffy soap box, and slightly mollified that I'd at least been invited, I acquiesce less than graciously to the offer of a lift, asking a little sullenly if he thinks Mabel will mind him taking Dotty. 'Well Pickles is coming, so I don't suppose one more will make much difference. Oscar'll be here in a jiffy, so go and get your coat if you're taking one.' He steps out, shutting the study door behind him as I hurry to grab a jacket. 'Just one more thing, Victory,' he shouts to my back as I start up the stairs, 'If you use that bloody tone with your actor, he's likely to throw you out on your ear.'

To my horror, Oscar's car turns out to be a nifty little sporty number and really only designed for two. Consequently, the back seat is more like a shelf. The top is also down, obviously taking advantage of the unusually clement weather. My nerves are strung like cheese wire, and the prospect of arriving at Noah's house in an open-top sports car with my knees hunched up around my neck, is really not helping matters at all.

Oscar himself is an affable looking man in his midtwenties with a plethora of tattoos decorating every exposed section of his body. 'When he dies, I wonder if he wants to be buried, cremated or framed,' my father mutters as he watches him jump nimbly out of the car. Stifling the urge to kick my rude insensitive parent, I content myself with giving him a quick glare, before plastering a smile on my face. Hopefully, Mabel's son was too far away to catch my father's little quip, or his hopes of marrying the merry widow this side of never will have taken a distinct turn for the worst.

I decide to take refuge in Dotty, always available to take the awkwardness out of any potentially embarrassing situation. Perhaps I should hire her out. I drop her lead and let her do her thing. Oscar is immediately entranced, obviously no more immune to Dotty's wiles than anyone else who has a penchant for cute furry things. Crouching down, he rubs her tummy as she rolls over delightedly. Unfortunately, Pickles's attempt to get in on the action is slightly less endearing as he dashes over and enthusiastically attempts to hump Oscar's back.

Five minutes later, we're off. As predicted, I'm folded into the back seat with Dotty squashed on the floor beside my feet. Dad is ensconced in the front passenger seat, but any feeling of authority he might have derived from that has been completely ruined by Pickles sitting practically on his head. The spaniel appears to be loving every second and is lifting his nose to the wind, panting excitedly. Unfortunately, the same wind is ensuring that the resulting slobber is blowing directly into my father's comb over. Still, it probably gives a better hold than *Brylcreem*. Dotty, on the other hand, is not so keen on the whole open-top car thing. I can feel her shivering from the depths of what is laughably called the rear foot well.

By the time we get through Kingswear and are onto the road winding round the headland, the enchanting, slightly tousled style I'd painstakingly managed to tease my hair into has now been replaced by a tangled unkempt mess. Unfortunately (or fortunately) I haven't bought a mirror, so as I get out of the car - after instructing Oscar to park it two hundred yards down the road (better to be safe than sorry) - I do my best to run my fingers through it in an effort to remove some of the tangles. Dotty tries desperately to follow me as I go to leave, so we waste another five minutes re-assigning the animal passengers.

By the time I start my hike up to Noah's house, Pickles is wedged into the back seat, and Dotty is sitting trembling in my father's lap. It's not ideal, and, as I walk, I can't help but torture myself with visions of my little dog throwing herself out of a moving vehicle in a desperate effort to get back to me. In my heart I know she really isn't that stupid (especially as I handed Dad a couple of treats to give her), but it definitely keeps me from hyperventilating over the prospect of my forthcoming meeting with Noah.

As I get closer to the house, my footsteps slow until I finally halt under a copse of trees about thirty yards away. My heart is now slamming against my ribs and for a minute or so, I'm really not sure I can actually go on. What on earth was I thinking? Why the bloody hell would Noah Westbrook, who could have any woman he wanted on the entire planet, want to take another chance on little old overanxious me?

Then I hear his voice in my head the last time we were together. *'You just don't understand that all of that Hollywood stuff – it's not real. What we had – me and you – that was real.'* And I think about tomorrow, how I'll feel if I never even tried. Unexpectedly, a sudden calm fills me. What's the worst that could happen? He throws me out, then sells the story to the newspapers. Big deal. Humiliation for a couple of weeks before the world moves on to the next juicy piece of gossip. I got through it the last time, and the time before that. I pause for a second wondering if there was actually a time before the time before that. Nope, only twice so far – a breeze.

I. Can. Do. This.

I square my shoulders, give my hair a last tease and march to Noah's front door with a lump the size of England in my throat.

Chapter Eighteen

As I raise my hand to ring the huge antique ship's bell hanging next to the front door, I pause for a second, helplessly feeling my eyes well up as I recall bringing it back one day from Kit's gallery. Noah had loved it and proclaimed it perfect. Oh God, don't let me start crying now. Furiously, I blink back the tears, and, taking a deep breath, ring the bell sharply before I get a chance to change my mind. Then I stand, heart thudding, hands nervously smoothing down my dress over and over, just to give them something to do. For a heart-stopping minute there is no sound from inside. Then I hear voices. And footsteps. Coming towards the door…

'Hey, great to…' The woman who throws open the door stumbles to a halt as she sees me. While obviously expecting someone, that someone is clearly not me. She frowns slightly, then her brow clears, and she steps forward. 'Can I help you?' she asks in a soft melodious voice. I just stare back at her and want to jump into the deepest, darkest hole I can find. She's simply the most beautiful woman I've ever seen. Long smooth chestnut hair frames a face that is both serene and seductive, and she gazes back at me with eyes the colour of clear water. Tall and willowy, she is absolutely everything I am not.

I have nothing to say. Nothing at all. All I can think is, I shouldn't have come. Stupid, stupid, stupid. As she raises her beautifully shaped eyebrows in enquiry, I finally open my mouth to mumble some kind of apology as I back up slowly, just wanting to escape.

In my haste to get away, I stumble slightly, and she steps forward, hand outstretched in a futile effort to halt my almost certain fall. Fortunately, I manage to avoid actually landing on my backside which would have been the icing on the cake as far as my total mortification is concerned, and as I struggle to right myself, she finally manages to take hold of my arm to steady me. My face is now the colour of a ripe tomato, and my mouth simply refuses to work at all. As she helps me regain my balance, she's looking at me with a slight frown as though she knows me from somewhere – which of course is impossible. I could never forget a face like hers.

Letting me go, she steps back, still frowning, and then all of a sudden, she smiles, and I feel as though I could gaze at her forever. After a second though, her words penetrate the cabbage that is currently my brain. 'You're Tory, aren't you?' Surprise renders me speechless (well it would've done if I'd actually said anything coherent), and without warning, she steps back into my personal space and bizarrely gives me a quick hug. All my poor brain can think is WTF? I feel like Jamie must have when he used his magic torch to helter skelter himself into Cuckoo Land.

'I'm Kim, Noah's sister,' she continues cheerfully. 'I didn't recognise you. You don't look anything like your photos.' I stare at her in disbelief as her words finally get through. Then I do the worst possible thing I could do. I laugh. Hysterically.

She visibly flinches at my maniacal cackling, no doubt wondering why Noah hasn't mentioned the fact that I'm a few grapes short of a fruit salad.

Finally, alarmed that I'm actually beginning to sound like an extra from a Vincent Price movie, I make a monumental effort to get my totally inappropriate hilarity under control. In the end however, all I can manage is a wheezing, 'Neither do you.' She's probably had more meaningful conversations with a brick wall. In a last-ditch effort to pull myself together, I bend over and begin rummaging through my handbag for a tissue. Unfortunately, the handbag fairy's been at it again, and all I come up with is a screwed-up piece of toilet paper.

Not daring to look back at the vision in front of me, I stare at the ground and attempt to wipe my runny nose on a piece of tissue the size of a stamp. As I dab futilely at each nostril, a string of snot from my nose determinedly clings to the remnants of the tissue until, like a toddler, I'm forced to wipe it away with the back of my hand. I can't begin to imagine what she must think of me, and with that thought, my unseemly hysterics finally subside, leaving a welcoming numbness in their wake.

Squeezing my hand around the sodden remains of the toilet paper, I look back up at the woman I'd once hoped would eventually be my sister. 'I'm so sorry,' I whisper, 'I'll – I'll leave now.' I turn away wondering if I have the nerve to complete my disgrace by making a run for it. However, as I take the first step, a hand takes hold of my arm again and I turn back.

'Why are you here?' Kim asks softly, searchingly. We stare at each other silently.

'I think you know,' is my eventual unsmiling response. Then I shake my head ruefully. 'I don't know what you must think of me,' I continue, echoing my earlier thought, 'I don't usually behave so erratically, it's just…' I wave my hand towards the still open door, and she nods her head in perfect understanding.

'Why don't you come in?' she says kindly, giving my arm a gentle tug.

'I'm not sure that's such a good idea,' I reply, trying to quash the sudden small surge of hope flickering inside me, 'You're obviously expecting guests.'

'One more won't make any difference.' She tugs at my arm again, this time drawing me close enough to tuck her hand into my elbow and tow me gently towards the open door.

'Despite any outward impression he may give, I think my brother will want to see you.' She pauses as the voice that has haunted my dreams shouts her name from the kitchen. 'Be right there, honey,' she answers, looking at me. Then, smiling mischievously, she pulls me towards the spiral staircase that dominates the hall. 'Come on, we'll give him a surprise,' she whispers, 'You can freshen up in my bedroom.'

As she leads the way, familiarity washes over me in a wave of nostalgic longing. How can I be homesick for a house I never fully lived in? We pass Noah's room, and the longing turns to an almost unbearable ache, until thankfully we turn down the guest corridor and enter the first bedroom. I know this room. I designed it with Kim in mind. As I turn to her, the question on my lips, she beats me to it. 'I love it,' she says simply, warmly, and I start to cry.

I've been hiding in Kim's bedroom for the last forty-five minutes, and I know I can't stay here much longer. I can hear voices talking and laughing downstairs, but the thought of making a grand entrance is practically giving me palpitations. I feel just like the first time Noah and I met at my father's impromptu dinner party – it seems like a lifetime ago.

Kim thoughtfully left me to compose myself after I broke down earlier, popping up under the cover of arriving guests to slip me a welcome glass of courage-inducing wine and to advise me with a quick grin to help myself to her make-up. One look in her bathroom mirror, and I almost groaned aloud. The image in front of me actually resembled Lady Gaga at her most eccentric. Since then, I've done what I can with my bird's nest hair and attempted to duplicate the fresh-faced outdoor look it took me bloody ages to achieve earlier. Now I'm sitting on the bed holding my empty glass of wine in a death grip and wondering what the hell I'm doing here.

In a panic, I hear footsteps coming along the corridor, and suddenly Kim sticks her head around the door. 'Wow, you look great,' is her encouraging assessment of the newly reinvented me. Then her next words have me swallowing convulsively. 'Come on, sweetie, you can't sit up here all night. Let's get this over with.' Her tone is warm and kind but firm, all at the same time, reminding me so much of her brother. Hesitantly I stand up.

'What if he really doesn't want to see me,' I stammer, glancing longingly at the window. Throwing myself out of it is looking pretty good right now.

'That's why I've hidden you up here until the last minute,' she chuckles, clearly enjoying herself. 'He won't make a scene and throw you out in front of the director of his next movie.'

'*What*,' I hiss. 'Oh God, I – I can't.' I sit back down on the bed feeling sick, prompting my tormentor to come into the room. She bends down in front of me, and her lovely eyes are sincere and sympathetic. 'Noah's told me so much about you, Tory. I know he's angry and hurt, but I really do believe that he hasn't stopped loving you. Are you really going to sit here because you're too frightened to take the chance that I'm right?'

Is she? I don't know any more. Biting my lip, I try to force down a terrible premonition of failure. If Noah truly still cared for me, wouldn't he have come to me before this? Oblivious to the battle going on inside me, Kim holds out her hand in invitation, and taking a deep breath, I stand up and place my fingers in hers.

Noah glanced down at his watch for the fifth time. Where the bloody hell was Kim? All the guests had arrived, and just listening to the laughter and noise was giving him a headache.

He needed his sister to deflect the small talk he was simply too weary to deal with. He looked around the drawing room. How he hated this house now. Everything in it reminded him of Tory. Now that he'd signed the deal for *Panic*, he was going to put the bloody thing on the market. He took a long swallow of his Champagne.

It was Kim's idea to hold a dinner party in Dartmouth to celebrate closing the damn deal, insisting that she simply had to see the house her brother had waxed so lyrically about before he finally sold it. Noah took another frustrated swallow of his drink. At this moment in time, he had absolutely no clue as to why he'd gone along with her harebrained idea.

'Noah, I've just finished speaking with your new director.' His agent Tim's words were full of suppressed excitement, much the same as when he'd told Noah about the disaster that was about to hit the Shackleford family. 'Peter believes this movie is going to make you *the* numero uno in Tinsel Town. Trust me, you're going to be the highest paid and most fucking sought after actor on the whole bloody planet.' He raised his Champagne glass, failing to see that his words were falling on deaf ears.

All Noah could see was his agent's gloating expression as he'd advised the actor to finish his relationship with Tory. It was very clear that Tim was basking in Noah's newly elevated status as the world's highest paid actor. To him, Tory had been an encumbrance, an embarrassment, and one to be got rid of at the earliest opportunity.

Well, his agent had turned out to be right. His popularity was soaring now he was single again. Noah raised his glass and smiled, but if there was no warmth in it, Tim was too single minded to notice. 'Are you looking forward to working with Peter?' The woman's voice purring in his ear belonged to the producer of *Panic*, who had made it very clear during the negotiations that as far as she was concerned, Noah was the only male lead she'd consider.

Repressing an urge to step away from the cloying scent now filling his nostrils, Noah turned towards Samantha Lewin, spoiled daughter of billionaire Ronald Lewin, and the major financer of the upcoming thriller. 'I couldn't be happier,' he murmured, making an effort to turn on the charm. It seemed to be working. Samantha's face slowly suffused with colour, and she caught her breath as Noah directed a slow sensual grin towards her. Then abruptly, the smile disappeared, and for a second she thought she'd done something wrong until she realized he was gazing over her shoulder at someone who had just come through the door.

All too quickly we get to the drawing room entrance. I can see about a dozen people milling about the room, and my heart somersaults as I remember the last party Noah held here. The one where he kissed me. My eyes automatically gravitate towards Noah, talking to a red-haired beauty who appears to be trying to eat him. His eyes are warm and inviting as he smiles at her to devastating effect. I almost feel sorry for her. Almost. Then he looks over his companion's shoulder towards the doorway – obviously waiting for Kim to appear.

I can tell the exact moment he catches sight of me. The smile leaves his expression, and his face closes completely. For a second, he stares at me, his beautiful eyes hooded and unreadable, then, just as I think he's going to ignore me altogether, he excuses himself and strides deliberately towards us.

Panicking, I cast a wild glance towards Kim, wondering if I should just bolt, but she places her hand on my arm again to hold me still as she faces down her clearly angry sibling. 'Is this your doing Kim?' he enquires coldly, deliberately ignoring the quivering emotional wreck that is me standing next to her.

Unnoticed, I stare at them both, wondering how I could ever have mistaken them for anything other than brother and sister. 'Noah, before you say anything you might regret,' Kim takes her arm from mine and places her hand urgently on her brother's shoulder before continuing in a low intense voice, 'Tory didn't come here at my invitation, she came because she wanted to speak to you.' I can see a vein throbbing in his neck, the only indication that he's furious with both of us.

'Is now really the time or the place?' he snaps, still as if I'm not there. His continuing rudeness shatters something inside of me, and abruptly, I've had enough, my anguish finally replaced with a welcome anger.

'Would you prefer that I make an appointment,' I enquire, equally frostily. His eyes snap back to me, and for a split second, I feel as if they're devouring me, hungry and intense. Then it's gone, replaced by a look of almost boredom, his eyes coolly regarding me as if I'm a tiresome acquaintance he simply has to tolerate occasionally. 'Stay if you wish,' he says finally, distantly. 'I'll get them to lay another place for dinner.' Then he turns on his heels and walks away.

I'm sat at the other end of the table to Noah during dinner and not once has he acknowledged my presence since briefly introducing me to the other guests as his interior designer. Of course, it's obvious that everyone present knows exactly who I am, and it doesn't make for a pleasant relaxing dining experience. As I struggle to deflect the mixture of comments tossed my way - some simply curious, others downright spiteful - I surreptitiously watch Noah exchange teasing, witty banter with the guests around him. As I listen to his familiar sexy laughter, I try to continue eating, but slowly, a lump of desolation is swelling in my throat.

I know Kim meant for me to see this to the end, but I know I can't. Noah clearly has no interest in finding out the reason for my sudden appearance. I finally acknowledge that it really is over, and the sooner I escape, the better. Feeling bruised and battered, I lift my napkin from my lap and place it down on the table beside my plate, before reaching down to slide my chair back.

'How is your father? It must be a great relief that he managed to wriggle out of a murder trial in Thailand.' I freeze. So far, everyone has at least had the good manners to avoid the topic of the recent allegations against my father. I stop sliding my chair and look up to a sea of eyes, all staring my way. I have no idea who's spoken. Frantically, I try to think of something to say, but before I can open my mouth, the voice continues, dripping sarcasm and spite. Feeling suddenly sick, I realize it belongs to Noah's agent.

'But then I suppose any publicity is better than none. Especially once your five minutes of fame are up.' I daren't look at Noah but shoot a quick glance towards Kim whose expression is a mixture of anger towards Tim and sympathy for me. Fighting the urge to shove my chair all the way back and simply flee, I finally look towards Noah. His anger at his agent's rudeness is palpable, his fingers gripping the wine glass as if he intends to break it. But his eyes are not on Tim, they're on me.

He wants to see what I'll do. He's expecting me to run away. In a nanosecond, my mind goes back to our many conversations about 'his world' and 'my world'. He can continue to protect me, deflecting every snide remark thrown at my door, while I sit and whine about not fitting in and obsessing about how other people see me. But rudeness is the same in any world. And it's not acceptable, (unless, of course, it's my father...)

Taking a deep breath, I transfer my gaze to Tim. His face is belligerent and hostile, his narrowed eyes telling me just how much he hates me, hates the fact that Noah was prepared to give up everything for a nobody. And a plain Jane at that.

'My father was cleared of all charges as I'm sure you know,' I say finally, shakily, 'And I'm not prepared to discuss the ins and outs of the case to someone who clearly has the manners of a three-year-old, and possibly the IQ of a deck chair. As for your insinuation that I was hanging on to Noah's coat tails to get my five minutes of fame, perhaps the analogy more accurately refers to yourself. But, as my father would no doubt say if he was here: As long as your arse points downwards, you'll always be a gopher. Now, if you'll excuse me...'

In the deathly silence that follows, I finally stand up from the table and walk quickly to the door without looking back.

I'm shaking with anger and grief by the time I reach the lobby leading to the front door, and all I can think of is getting out. Unfortunately, my desperate haste is making it difficult to work the lock that will get me to freedom. As I fumble with the catch, almost crying with frustration, an achingly familiar voice behind me stops me in my tracks.

'Why did you come here, Tory?'

There's a brief silence as I stare at the obstinate lock, then without moving, I say hesitantly, 'I – I would have thought it was obvious.'

'No, actually, it isn't. Would you care to enlighten me?' His voice is giving nothing away, and in the end, I turn round, needing to see for myself whether he really does want to know why I'm here, when all the evidence up to now screams that he doesn't care. He's leaning against the doorframe at the entrance to the hall. The lamp behind him is casting shadows over the inky blackness of his hair, blurring his features in the dimness of the lobby. I want to ask him to turn the light on so I can see the expression in his eyes, but then maybe it's better, easier to do it like this.

I take a deep, steadying breath. 'I – I wanted to tell you that you were right. The problem *was* me, not the situation,' I say finally in a small voice, stuttering slightly in my effort to make him understand. 'I used the allegations against my father as an excuse to drive you away. I told myself you'd be better off without me - that I was saving you.' I give a small mirthless laugh, 'But the real truth is that I simply couldn't accept that I was enough for you, *as I am* - that you wanted *me*. It didn't make any sense,' I whisper finally. 'No-one could *ever* consider me to be movie star girlfriend material.'

'And now?' His voice cracks slightly, the only sign that my answer is important to him.

'Now it doesn't matter.'

Noah's whole body tenses as he absorbs the meaning of my words, and for a horrible second I wonder if I've got it all wrong. Then he pushes himself away from the frame and walks slowly towards me, eyes never leaving mine, only stopping when his shirt is inches away from my breasts. I can feel the heat of him through the thin material, and my heart thuds erratically in response.

'What took you so long?' he finally whispers huskily, before pulling me into his arms and crushing me to his chest, his mouth at long last closing hungrily over mine.

With a small moan of joy, I surrender completely to his kiss, pressing myself against the hard length of him and glorying in the feel of his lips against mine. I twine my arms around his neck as he pulls me closer, hands molding me to him, sliding up my spine, then lower, gathering my willing body into his. 'God how I've missed you,' he breathes hoarsely against my lips, before deepening the kiss.

'What the fuck are you doing? Have you lost your mind,

Noah?' The harsh voice penetrates, finally breaking our kiss, and reluctantly, Noah steps away from me, keeping me shielded behind him as he turns towards the intruder. 'I think you've said enough Tim,' he says evenly to his enraged agent, standing at the entrance to the hall.

'The hell I have,' Tim responds in a low furious tone. 'Is this some kind of fucking game Noah – is that it? See how many times you can bang the wallflower?' Noah takes a warning step forward, squeezing my hand briefly before pushing me gently away as I try to hold him back.

'*Enough.*' I'm not the only one who flinches at the tightly controlled fury in his voice. Tim pauses in midtirade, shocked at Noah's icy tone. He takes a step back as the actor walks purposefully towards him. 'You and I are done, Tim. Finished,' he spits out in a harsh voice I hardly recognise. 'But unless you want to be thrown out in front of Hollywood's finest, I suggest you return to the dining table and make nice. Once dinner is over, I'll call you a cab.'

'I – I … you can't *do* this, you ungrateful bastard,' his agent sputters, a look of incredulity on his face. 'You were a nobody when I took you on. I made you what you are today. I *own* you.' I draw in my breath, watching Noah's hands tighten into fists, truly frightened now that he'd do something he might regret. But after a couple of seconds, his fingers unclench, and he comes back from the brink, saying calmly,

'You've been paid very handsomely for your services, Tim, but *nobody* owns me, and you of all people should know that. I love Tory, and I *will* marry her. My private life is my own - it has *nothing* to do with you or anybody else. Now, get the fuck out of my face.'

I stopped listening at "marry". Noah Westbrook wants to marry me. OMG…

Tim opens his mouth to reply, but one look at his former employer's set features, changes his mind. Face flaming, he turns abruptly on his heels and heads back to the dining room, leaving us alone again in the lobby. We stare at each other for a couple of seconds, then Noah beckons me to him, and as I reach his side, he folds me in his arms with a sigh.

'I think you should go back to your guests,' I finally mumble reluctantly, wanting nothing more than to stay here, safe in his arms, forever. His answer is to tip my chin up to look at him before saying quietly, 'Are you willing to marry me Tory?'

I nod my head, finding it so hard to speak round the sudden lump in my throat. Then, knowing he needs to hear me say it, I swallow convulsively and place my hand gently against his cheek before whispering, 'Yes.'

You might be wondering, given my dramatic exit, whether I accompanied Noah back to the dinner table. The answer is yes. For some reason, Noah seems reluctant to let me out of his sight, announcing arbitrarily that I will be living in this house from tonight. I know he has to return to Ireland in a couple of days to wrap up filming *Nocturne*, so I allow him to boss me around. Tomorrow morning, we'll go together to tell my father and our friends.

But tonight is ours. As we return to the dining room, Noah actually has the caterers move my seat next to his before announcing brazenly to the rest of the assembly that I've had a promotion. I can tell the whole table is waiting with bated breath to see if he'll elaborate – including me. But he leaves everyone guessing. I think he's intending to show me later exactly what my new job entails...

I'm done hiding in the shadows, fixated with other people's ideas of who I should be. I finally know who I am. I am Victory Britannia Shackleford, soon to be Westbrook.

I am me.

Epilogue

Charles Shackleford was a contented man. Life was going swimmingly – not that it was all due to chance, of course. His firm philosophy was that you only got out of life what you put into it – and in the Admiral's book, that meant interfering whenever necessary. Mabel had agreed to shack up with him, providing they made it legal pretty sharpish, and, the icing on the cake? He'd been invited to a Royal Garden Party at Buckingham Palace no less. So here he was, hob-knobbing in a posh hotel with Mabel, both of them about to get their glad rags on to go and meet the Queen. Charles Shackleford didn't think it could get any better than this.

To be fair, he had no idea why he'd been invited, especially as the invitation had only arrived a few days ago. This particular garden party was actually an addition to the usual shindigs held at the Palace during the early summer, but the reason for it was another mystery. He didn't actually like to ask, just in case his invitation turned out to be a mistake.

While Mabel commandeered the en-suite, the Admiral struggled into his uniform - jacket, gold laced trousers and blue waistcoat. The last time he'd worn this get up was for the bloody premier of *The Bridegroom* in Leicester Square. He'd gone as far as having the whole lot cleaned afterwards (the smell of mothballs seemed to put some people off) and he was now convinced it had shrunk. Puffing and panting, he finally managed to get the whole ensemble on, and observing himself in the mirror he couldn't help but reflect what a fine figure of a man he still was – emphasized by Mabel's admiring comments as she finally emerged from the bathroom. 'We certainly look the business, Mabel old girl,' he said finally, and picking up his cap, he ushered his bride-to-be out of the hotel room.

Twenty minutes later, they arrived at Buckingham Palace, joining the queue of people waiting to get into the royal gardens. As they stood in line, the Admiral actually felt a little miffed. He had no idea there would be all these bloody people – there must be a few thousand. What chance would he and Mabel have to meet Her Royal Highness in this bloody cake and arse party? Still, as they shuffled forward, he contented himself with the knowledge that, if nothing else, an invitation like this would definitely see him in the local paper.

It was another half an hour before they finally got into the Palace gardens but there was no time to relax as almost immediately the National Anthem signified the arrival of the Queen. As Mabel twittered next to him, the Admiral kept his eyes peeled to see if there was anybody he recognised. They were ushered into rows, and the Admiral waited with bated breath to see which Royal they would be introduced to. This would keep him in beer at the Ship until at least Christmas.

Suddenly, in the distance, he could see her majesty as she slowly began making her way towards them. *Yes.* The Admiral felt a swelling of patriotic pride as he waited in line, abstractly wondering whether Mabel had ever curtsied before. Craning his neck in an effort not to miss anything, he gradually became aware of a man in civilian clothes walking slightly behind the Queen, to her right. He definitely looked familiar. As the party drew closer, the Admiral frowned, Her Royal Highness briefly forgotten, as he struggled to remember where he'd seen the man before. Until, finally the Queen was there, directly in front of them. As she stopped and smiled, Charles Shackleford bowed, murmuring, 'Your Majesty,' as he'd been instructed. Then, straightening up, he looked directly into the eyes of Doris.

There could be no mistake. He might look older, but it was definitely Doris Day. The Admiral stared with an open mouth as the Queen slowly moved past them. Then, unbelievably, the former sub lieutenant turned back towards him and winked. Who the hell was he? The Admiral tried making discreet enquiries to the people standing next to him, but nobody seemed to have a clue. Later, in the tea tent, he tried again, but everyone he questioned seemed to have only had eyes for the members of the Royal Family. The men who accompanied them appeared to be almost invisible.

The Admiral saw the Queen once more from a distance as she left the festivities, but although he strained, he couldn't see whether Doris was still with her. Disappointed, he distractedly took Mabel's arm, and they made their way towards the entrance.

As they arrived back at the hotel and were crossing the lobby, he was so deep in thought that, at first, he didn't realize that someone was blocking their path. Looking up he saw a woman he remembered seeing at the reception desk earlier. 'Are you Charles Shackleford?' she asked politely but impersonally. At the Admiral's nod, she thrust out her hand holding a small cream-coloured envelope. 'I think this is for you, Sir,' she continued, handing him the missive. The Admiral looked around wildly.

'Who – who gave it to you?' he asked urgently.

'It was left at the desk about five minutes ago, Mr. Shackleford,' was her infuriating answer, 'Now if you'll excuse me, I have other guests to check in.'

The Admiral pulled Mabel aside, next to the lift, and with trembling hands he opened the envelope and drew out the letter inside. There were just a few lines.

Hope you enjoyed the Royal Garden Party, Charlie. The invitation was my way of saying thank you. I wish I could have done more.

It was good to see you looking so well after all this time, and who knows, we might bump into one another again at some future cake and arse party...

Until then, I remain

Yours aye

Doris

THE END

Do you want to find out why the most famous film star in the world fell for an ordinary girl?

Falling For Victory tells the story of Claiming Victory from Noah's point of view. Find out how and why he fell in love with Tory...

Sign up to my newsletter by copying and pasting the link below into your browser and I'll send you a FREE digital copy of *Falling For Victory*

https://motivated-teacher-3299.ck.page/d68eed985f

If you enjoyed Sweet Victory, you may be interested to know that *All For Victory* - Book Three of The Dartmouth Diaries, *Chasing Victory* – Book Four, Lasting Victory: Book Five and *A Shackleford Victory* - Book Six – are now available on Amazon in both ebook and paperback.

Keep reading for an exclusive sneak peek of All For Victory: Book Three of The Dartmouth Diaries...

Author's Note

As I mentioned in Claiming Victory, if you ever find yourself in the South West of England, it is truly worth your while to take some time to visit the beautiful yachting haven of Dartmouth.

If you'd like more information about the town and the surrounding areas, here's a link to the Tourist Information Centre:

https://discoverdartmouth.com

And the second location in Sweet Victory...?

Loch Long in the glorious Scottish Highlands does exist – although I've yet to come across Bloodstone Tower! The loch itself is a beautiful sea loch surrounded by mountains. It forms the entire western coastline of the Rosneath Peninsula in Western Scotland, an area so magnificent it will take your breath away...

For more information about Loch Long and the Rosneath Peninsula, copy and paste the link below:

http://www.trossachs.co.uk/loch-long.php

Just in case you were completely baffled, here's a list of the Scottish phrases used by Aileen in Sweet Victory, along with their meanings...

Awrite, guid mornin, nice tae meit ye: Hi, good morning, nice to meet you.

A hae tae gang, a'll be reit back: I have to go, I'll be right back.
Haur ye gae: Here you go.

Haud yer wheesht: Be quiet

Ah, guid eenin: Hi, good evening.

Hou's aw wi ye: How are you?

Och ye scunner, watch ma tatties: Oh you clumsy thing, watch my potatoes.

Tatties o'wer the side and no mistake hen: It's all gone wrong/ disaster's struck my dear.

Keep the heid: Keep calm and don't lose your head.

It's gaein be awricht ance the pain has gane awa: As soon as that pesky bad stuff is out of the way, everything will be fine.

Och, ye numpty, ah pure wallaped ma heid aff that bloody shelf: Oh, you idiot, I hit my head on the shelf.

All For Victory

Chapter One

It's not often that a fledgling career in event management kicks off with the wedding of a Hollywood superstar. Of course, the fact that this particular Hollywood star is marrying my best friend might have had something to do with the fact that little old me landed the job.

It's amazing just how things can change in the blink of an eye. Two months ago, I was the owner of a small but very successful gallery here in Dartmouth. However, unfortunately the word *owner* didn't actually include the property the gallery was housed in, which was (and still is – just) owned by my self-absorbed and largely absent parents.

Until a month ago, I hadn't actually seen them for five years, and before that only sporadically.

Just after my fourteenth birthday, they left me in the care of my dad's sister Florence while they *travelled.* Mum had inherited a substantial amount of property in Dartmouth – even back then, it fetched a premium - and over the years, they sold each one until there was only the property on Fore Street left. My gallery.

Dad said they needed to sell it so he and mum could do true justice to South America – after all, travelling on a budget is no fun at all. He made it clear that he thought they were doing me a favour – giving me the push I needed to get a proper job.

I have to say it feels more like a kick in the nuts (or I'm sure it would if I had any).

I'm trying very hard not to be bitter, telling myself that everything happens for a reason.

By the time my parents finally arrived back in Dartmouth after dropping their little bombshell, I'd managed to sell most of my stock, so when they visited me at the gallery, I suppose their image of a daughter playing at being an entrepreneur seemed justified. But then, they really don't know anything about me.

Don't get me wrong, life as a teenager with Aunt Flo was the best part of my childhood; for one thing, it was never, ever dull.

My Aunt Flo is a well-known author of romantic bodice rippers, which she thankfully writes under a pen name, as her books generally abound with heaving bosoms and throbbing members.

By the time I left school, I knew at least twenty different words for penis in three different languages...

She was, and still is the most wonderful loving person, and I know she adores me. Plus, I have Victory, my best friend since forever, and the soon to be wife of multimillionaire Hollywood golden boy Noah Westbrook.

Which of course is why, when it looked as though I was about to become homeless and penniless, she announced that she wanted me to plan her wedding.

There is one other teensy-weensy reason that I've landed the job that wedding planners everywhere can only dream of – one that only Noah and I know about.

Tory is pregnant.

Apparently, it happened on the night of their big reconciliation just over six weeks ago...

Now, delighted they both are, but here's the kicker. Noah is refusing to wait until after the birth to make an honest woman of her. (To be fair, I can't blame him. Tory is my dearest and oldest friend, and I love her to pieces, but it has to be said she has a disturbing tendency to make life difficult for herself, and consequently everyone around her.)

So, Noah is determined that the wedding will go ahead before he begins filming his next movie in the spring– even if he has to drag her to the altar.

Tory has absolutely refused to be a bride with a bump – citing the fact that her father would have a coronary. We are of course talking about the Admiral here, who's a stickler for protocol when it comes to anyone other than himself.

So, the wedding has to be pre-bump and is tentatively planned for the twentieth of December.

Seven weeks away...

Of course, the Admiral is insisting on full pomp and ceremony for his only daughter, which means he wants the whole shebang held up at Britannia Royal Naval College which he presided over as Commodore for a brief, though apparently memorable, period.

So, just to recap and make sure you're in the loop so to speak. I am being asked to organize a wedding in seven weeks' time with approximately one hundred and fifty guests - including several Hollywood A listers, as well as anyone who's anyone in *Hello* magazine – all to be held in a naval establishment requiring full details of every single guest down to what they had for breakfast, as well as the names and addresses of all their ancestors going back to the Middle Ages.

And I've never done it before.

Still, never let it be said that I don't like a challenge, and at least it's stopping me thinking about my woes.

Who knows, it could well lead to an exciting new career. If I don't balls it up in the meantime as the Admiral would say.

∞∞∞

It had just started to rain as Admiral Charles Shackleford (retired) finally opened the door of his favourite watering hole. Before striding into the bar at the Ship Inn, he glanced down to see exactly where his dog Pickles was.

The Springer Spaniel had recently developed an irritating habit of getting under the Admiral's feet which had caused him to go embarrassingly arse over tit a few times in polite company. Anyone would think the bloody dog was worried about being left behind.

Pickles, however, was way ahead of him, happily fussing round the small man already seated at the bar. Jimmy Noon looked up as his oldest friend made his way noisily to his usual seat.

Huffing and puffing, Charles Shackleford hoisted himself up onto the stool. It had to be said, this ritual was getting a trifle difficult – the Admiral admitted privately to himself that he might have put on a smidgeon of weight. Mabel had been threatening to put him on a diet. Bit of a bloody cheek since it was her cooking that had caused the sorry state of affairs in the first place. Never had any problem with putting on weight when Victory was cooking.

'How are you, Sir?' Jimmy interrupted his maudlin reverie, and

SWEET VICTORY: A ROMANTIC COMEDY

the Admiral sighed before taking a long draft of his pint, ready and waiting for him.

'Would you believe the damn wedding's been brought forward to December,' he responded finally after putting his glass back onto the bar. 'December, I ask you. What's wrong with having a decent length of time to plan the bloody thing properly?'

Jimmy frowned, a little perplexed at the Admiral's attitude. 'What's wrong with that?' he asked with a bewildered shrug. 'I know it's a bit quick, but it's not like you've got to organize it, and come on, Sir. It's good news really. Now you and Mabel won't have to wait so long to do the necessaries.'

The Admiral glared down at his friend before sighing again. It wasn't Jimmy's fault that he'd gone and got himself in a bit of a tight spot. Of course, the problem was, as usual, that he was too charitable for his own good.

The Admiral took another drink of his pint while he debated whether to just come out with it. He wasn't sure exactly what Jimmy would be able to muster up to salvage the situation, especially given the fact that his best friend would be inclined to lose a debate with a doorknob. Still, it had to be said that Jimmy was probably the only person he *could* speak to about the slight issue. Well, either him or Pickles.

After a couple of minutes meditating into his pint, the Admiral plonked his glass onto the bar decisively before turning determinedly towards the smaller man. 'The thing is, Jimmy lad, you know me. Sometimes, I'm just too bloody giving for my own good.'

Jimmy stared silently back at him with his glass poised halfway to his mouth. The Admiral waited a second for his friend's agreement, but after a few seconds, it appeared Jimmy had lost the use of his tongue. Not the first time it had happened.

Sometimes, he privately thought that his former master at arms might not actually have both oars in the water. So, frowning slightly, he continued.

'Well, a couple of weeks ago, I had a phone call from that amen wallah – you know, the one who used to be chaplain up at the College when I first signed up?'

Jimmy frowned. 'You mean Bible Basher Boris? The one with the terrible flatulence problem? I thought he died years ago.'

'Well, it has to be said, so did I,' responded the Admiral glumly. 'Then he just popped out of the woodwork a few months ago. He must be ninety if he's a day. Thing is, he's heard about Noah and Victory and put two and two together…'

'Well, that's nice of him,' Jimmy mused taking a sip of his pint. There was a certain measure of relief in his response, but he couldn't help wondering what on earth his meddling friend was getting so worked up about. 'Perhaps he wanted to buy them a present. Did you tell him about the wedding? I thought we were all supposed to keep schtum about it.'

'No, he didn't want to buy them a bloody present,' the Admiral replied irritably. 'Thing is, old Boris did me a bit of a favour a few years ago – got me out of a spot of bother so to speak.'

Jimmy's heart started its familiar thumping, and he held his breath, sensing that Charles Shackleford was about to deliver the punch line. He closed his eyes, waiting to see what disaster the Admiral had got himself into this time.

'Well, of course when he got me out of this tight spot, I was suitably grateful, and, well… Come on, Jimmy lad, you know how sentimental I am.' He paused for a reaction, but for some reason Jimmy was sitting with his eyes shut, so, shaking his head slightly, he ploughed on.

'Well, our Victory was only a few weeks old at the time, and in the heat of the moment, I sort of promised him he could do the business when she got married.'

'Do the business, what business?' Jimmy opened his eyes up again with a frown.

'I promised him he could marry her.'

'You said he could marry her? Oh, Sir, why on earth did you say that? She's marrying Noah.'

'What the bloody hell are you talking about, Jimmy? Have you finally lost your marbles?' The Admiral was now waving his hands about in agitation. 'I didn't say he could be her bollocking husband, I said he could take the ceremony. He's a God walloper isn't he?'

'But, Sir, he's got that awful wind problem.' Jimmy's response was a disbelieving whisper. 'You know he once cleared out the Old Naval Chapel at Greenwich.' Then he paused slightly before going on to hammer the final nail in the coffin, 'Have you told Tory?'

The Admiral opened his mouth to speak, then sighed and shook his head mournfully before taking another swallow of his pint. Then, despondently staring into its amber depths, he said finally, 'No, I thought there was no sense in sticking a bloody spanner in the works when we had months to go 'til the damn nuptials, and chances were old Boris would've had the decency to pop his clogs in the meantime.

'But now, well, now we've got seven bloody weeks. And he's unlikely to cash in his chips before then.'

'Well, why don't you just tell him he can't do the ceremony?' Jimmy responded reasonably. 'I'm sure he'll understand. After all, he's pretty ancient. Probably be too much for him anyway.'

'If only it was that simple, Jimmy lad,' the Admiral replied sorrowfully. 'The problem is, he says he's got his heart set on seeing my daughter wed properly. When he spoke to me, he said that doing this wedding would be his life's pinnacle, and once he'd done it, he could die happy.

'And I promised him, Jimmy, on my mother's grave. And you know what a sensitive soul I am, so how the bloody hell do I break it to him that he can't live out his lifelong dream because of his anal acoustics...'

So, here I am, brand spanking new filofax in hand battling my way up through the gates at BRNC with what feels like a ten-force gale trying its best to bring me to my knees. So much for the up-to-now glorious autumn weather.

I have an appointment with the Captain of the Naval College to talk about my best friend's upcoming nuptials and to discuss the detailed plan I have to avoid the whole thing turning into a media circus.

The problem is, I don't have one. Not yet. But as I've already postponed this meeting twice, I can't do it again.

So I spent all last night (and I mean *all*) trying to work out just how we're going to manage it. By three o'clock I hadn't even come up with a preliminary strategy. The sad fact is that I'm so far out of my depth the fishes have lights on their noses.

The trouble is Tory thinks it's all in hand. She *trusts* me. Oh God...

I've dressed extra carefully this morning – might as well look the part at least. I've exchanged my customary jeans and t-shirt for a business-like skirt and blouse.

Before leaving my flat, I stared critically at myself in the mirror. I had my hair cut a couple of weeks ago into a short pixie crop with some funky gold highlights. I thought it looked pretty cool, and Tory said she loved it. However, Freddy - our local guru of all things fashionable, insisted that the look was more reminiscent of an extra out of *The Hobbit.*

At the time I thought he was being bitchy, but looking at myself before leaving for a hugely important meeting, I could actually see his point.

I'm suddenly very glad my outfit isn't green.

I'm given a pass at the College Gate by a guard, who after having a few minutes of every word being swallowed by the howling gale, resorts to pointing at the visitor's book and handing me a pen to fill in my details.

As I hang my temporary ID card around my neck, I shout to confirm that Captain Taylor is expecting me. Unfortunately, his reply is pretty much lost in the storm, so I simply wave my thanks and pass through the gate, tucking my head into the collar of my jacket, in an effort to lessen the impact of the gale and concentrate on putting one foot in front of the other.

I've been inside the College grounds several times, and normally I enjoy the walk up the hill, with the beautiful Edwardian red brick building of the Naval College towering above me on one side and the breathtaking view of the River Dart below me on the other. Today however, the part of me not quaking in my shoes at the thought of the upcoming meeting is doing its best to keep said shoes on my feet.

Up to now the weather has been lovely, carrying on from the

fabulously hot summer we enjoyed. This year's autumn colours have been amazing with the leaves drifting down from the trees in a gradual cascade of red, yellow and orange.

As I fight my way up the path, I can't help but reflect that today's blustery weather might have seen off the last of autumn and plunged us kicking and screaming into winter.

By the time I finally reach the turn off to the Captain's house at the top of the hill, I feel as though I've done a marathon, and pause in the drive for a quick breather, and a chance to restore some semblance of order to my hair, which I suspect now bears more resemblance to a gonk than an elf.

Standing in the shade of a large azalea bush protecting me from the worst of the wind, I notice a white Audi TT in the drive next to the house. Somehow it looks familiar, as though I've seen it somewhere before. I frown, racking my brains for a second before dismissing the notion. It's not as though Audis are a rarity.

Taking a deep breath, I tuck my filofax under my arm and march determinedly towards the large front door before I have the chance to lose my nerve and run back down the hill.

I can hear the bell ringing somewhere deep in the house, and mentally, I rehearse my excuses – mainly focusing on the idea that I'm currently working on several different approaches to the problem (which is true really – I'm definitely working on them, it's just that none of them make any sense as of yet).

A couple of minutes later, the door is opened by what appears to be a butler. Bloody hell, it's like stepping into Downton Abbey. After leading me into a large central hallway, obviously serving as the main avenue of traffic and entrance area to the adjacent rooms, the butler (if that's who he is) politely asks me to take a seat, then promptly disappears. Sitting gingerly on one of the formal chairs up against the wall, my nerves lessen slightly as I look around me with interest.

The hallway flows into a large wide staircase, and everywhere are paintings and memorabilia depicting our glorious naval history. It's all very queen and country – in fact it all looks very similar to Tory's house. I can so picture the Admiral ensconced in this building and can't help but smother a grin at the mayhem he probably caused while he was here.

'The Captain will see you now.' I jump at the quiet voice abruptly coming from the entrance to what I assume is the drawing room. I've no idea how he got there, he left through a door in the other direction.

Heart suddenly pounding, I hurriedly get to my feet, feeling as though I'm heading towards my execution. 'For pity's sake, get a grip, girl,' I tell myself sternly as I cross the hall. 'He's not bloody royalty.' Mentally, I go over his name – Captain John Taylor. With a nod I step past the butler, my hand already held out in preparation. 'Captain Tay...' I start with an artificial smile plastered on my face, only to sputter to a halt as the man facing the window turns towards me and my eyes meet the icy, silver gaze of Jason Buchannan.

**All For Victory is available in ebook and
paperback from Amazon.**

Keeping in Touch

Thank you so much for reading *Sweet Victory*, I really hope you enjoyed it.

For any of you who'd like to connect, I'd really love to hear from you. Feel free to contact me via my facebook page: https://www.facebook.com/beverleywattsromanticcomedyauthor or my website: http://www.beverleywatts.com

If you'd like me to let you know as soon as my next book is available and receive your free ebook - *Falling For Victory* - sign up to my newsletter and I'll send you the ebook and keep you updated about all my latest releases.

https://motivated-teacher-3299.ck.page/d68eed985f

And lastly, thanks a million for taking the time to read this story. As I mentioned earlier, if you've not yet had your fill of the Admiral's meddling in the Dartmouth Diaries, Book Three: *All For Victory*, Book Four: *Chasing Victory* Book Five: *Lasting Victory* and Book 6: *A Shackleford Victory* are also available on Amazon, with Book Seven: *Final Victory* to be released on 13th December 24.

Additionally I have a series of cosy mysteries involving the Admiral and Jimmy, aptly titled *The Admiral Shackleford Mysteries.*

Book One: *A Murderous Valentine*, Book Two: *A Murderous Marriage* and Book Three: *A Murderous Season* are all available on Amazon.

SWEET VICTORY: A ROMANTIC COMEDY

You might also be interested to learn that the Admiral's Great, Great, Great, Great, Great Grandfather appears in my latest series of lighthearted Regency Romances entitled The Shackleford Sisters.

Book One: *Grace*, Book Two: *Temperance*, Book Three: *Faith*, Book Four: *Hope*, Book Five: *Patience*, Book Six: *Charity*, Book Seven *Chastity*, Book 8: *Prudence* and Book 9: *Anthony* are currently available on Amazon.

Turn the page for a full list of my books available on Amazon.

Books available on Amazon

The Dartmouth Diaries:

Book 1 - Claiming Victory

Book 2 - Sweet Victory

Book 3 - All for Victory

Book 4 - Chasing Victory

Book 5 - Lasting Victory

Book 6 - A Shackleford Victory

Book 7 - Final Victory now available for pre-order

The Shackleford Sisters

Book 1- Grace

Book 2 - Temperance

Book 3 - Faith

Book 4 - Hope

Book 5 - Patience

Book 6 - Charity

Book 7 - Chastity

Book 8 - Prudence

Book 9 - Anthony

The Shackleford Legacies

Book 1 - Jennifer

Book 2 - Mercedes now available for pre-order

The Admiral Shackleford Mysteries

Book 1 - A Murderous Valentine

Book 2 - A Murderous Marriage

Book 3 - A Murderous Season

Standalone Titles

An Officer and a Gentleman Wanted

About The Author

Beverley Watts

Beverley spent 8 years teaching English as a Foreign Language to International Military Students in Britannia Royal Naval College, the Royal Navy's premier officer training establishment in the UK. She says that in the whole 8 years there was never a dull moment and many of her wonderful experiences at the College were not only memorable but were most definitely 'the stuff of fiction.' Her debut novel An Officer And A Gentleman Wanted is very loosely based on her adventures at the College.

Beverley particularly enjoys writing books that make people laugh and currently she has two series of Romantic Comedies, both contemporary and historical, as well as a humorous cosy mystery series under her belt.

She lives with her husband in an apartment overlooking the sea on the beautiful English Riviera. Between them they have 3 adult children and two gorgeous grandchildren plus a menagerie of animals including 4 dogs - 3 Romanian rescues of indeterminate breed called Florence, Trixie, and Lizzie, and a 'Chichon" named Dotty who was the inspiration for Dotty in The Dartmouth Diaries.

You can find out more about Beverley's books at www.beverleywatts.com

Printed in Great Britain
by Amazon

46174067R00119